# My Heart Belongs in

# Tombstone,

# Arizona

## Heart of the Frontier

Book ♡ Two

# Samantha Bayarr

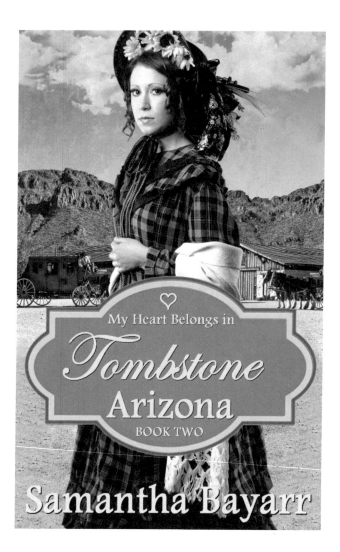

My Heart Belongs in

*Tombstone*

Arizona

BOOK TWO

Samantha Bayarr

# My Heart Belongs in

## Tombstone,

## Arizona

### Heart of the Frontier

Book ♡ Two

# Samantha Bayarr

This novel is a work of fiction set in a true community of El Paso, Texas in the 1860's and Tombstone, Arizona, in the 1880's. Although extensive research was done to preserve authenticity, some places, events, and circumstances are not documented at great length, therefore allowing the leeway of imagination to fill in some of the blanks. This book is intended for entertainment purposes only and should not to be used as a reference to the history of either city or historical timeline.

# Table of Contents

Is Beatrix, the new schoolmarm, leading a double life as a saloon girl named Trixie?

When Beatrix arrives in Tombstone thinking she's taking the position as the new school teacher, she's shocked to discover the invitation from the schoolmaster was for a mail-order bride instead. Having misunderstood his intentions, she rejects his offer of marriage; he leaves town and his position as the school teacher.
When the menfolk in town start to call her Trixie and rumors begin to fly, it isn't long before the entire town begins to accuse Beatrix of leading a double life. Little does she know that sheriff Muley Ransome, whom she's courting, has been investigating the strange coincidences that involve her. This includes the recent stagecoach robbery. Will he be able to save her reputation and their blossoming courtship, or does his investigation turn up more than they both bargained for?

## ONE

*El Paso, Texas, 1864*

Maxine Donovan rushed down the muddy street toward the midwife's clapboard house at the far end of town. Pale moonlight filtering through the scattered clouds reflected off the puddles from recent rains that filled the deep grooves in the road made from wagon wheels. The stench of manure mixed in with the mud, and there was very little she could do to avoid it; her boots had kicked it up as she ran, splattering the hem of her dress. Usually, she would tip-toe over the dirty street if she crossed it at all, but Verdie was in trouble, and there was no time to worry about the mud—or the manure.

In front of the white-washed, two-story home, she unlatched the gate of the white, picket fence, letting it swing back into the flower bed. Not bothering to clean her feet on the small patch of grass in the yard, she bounded up the wooden steps with muddy feet; she had no time to be quiet or to observe the late hour; the midwife's services were needed at once.

"Miss Maisy, Miss Maisy, Verdie needs you," she called out, her breath heaving, as she hammered against the screen door with her fist.

The door opened just a crack, but Maxine caught a glimpse of disgust in the eyes of the midwife's mother when she held up a lantern. The lamplight illuminated Maxine's bosom that spilled out from her low-cut, red dress and the bright light made her suddenly aware of how she must look to the tight-lipped woman. She'd neglected to grab a shawl to cover herself; instead, she'd run straight from the room above the saloon that she shared with her coworker, Verdie Wade.

"I'm sorry to come calling at such a late hour, but I need Miss Maisy to come quickly; Verdie needs her."

The old woman pursed her lips. "Even if she were here, I wouldn't allow her to step foot into the house of sin—not even to birth that baby. She has a reputation to maintain."

Maxine's knee-jerk reaction was to throw an insult the old woman's way, but Verdie needed the woman's help since the doctor left town without a word, and the town council had not yet been able to find another doctor. Besides, she liked Miss Maisy, and her retort would insult her more than it would her mother. It wasn't her place to remind the old woman that it was too late to protect her spinster daughter's reputation; her season had come and gone, despite the hope her aging mother held onto that Miss Maisy would find herself a husband.

"Where can I find her?" Maxine asked, still out of breath from running all the way there. "Verdie really needs her help—even if you don't approve."

"Mr. Pruett came to get her just moments ago to help his *wife* birth their child."

Maxine's face twisted up at the way the old woman emphasized the Pruetts' marital status.

"Verdie was married, and you know it, you old crow," she said, unable to contain her anger any longer. "She can't help it if she's a widow."

The old woman lifted her chin and rolled her eyes to the side. "One should expect to become a widow by marrying an outlaw; the man was doomed to be shot or hung sooner or later."

Maxine planted her hands on her hips and scowled at the old woman. "You have no idea what Verdie went through having to stand by— pregnant, and watching her husband hang while the folks in this town cheered," she said through gritted teeth. "But that don't change the fact that she needs help birthing her baby, and I don't know how to do that, so tell me where the Pruett farm is so I can fetch Miss Maisy to help Verdie."

"She won't be leaving the Pruetts' farm until their baby has been born, so you'll have to help that *soiled dove* yourself!"

The old woman closed the door in her face, and Maxine pounded against the screen once more. "It's a good thing your daughter doesn't share your hatred for others, you old crow!"

She ambled down the steps and ran out into the muddy street once more and headed toward the undertaker's place. Mr. Eddie had a buckboard, and he knew everyone in town; lucky for her, he would still be up at this hour. He would help her get Verdie out to the Pruett farm before it was too late.

From across the street, she spotted the older, rail-thin man leaning against the door frame of his building smoking a cigar, and wearing only a pair of long-johns, a tattered Stetson that was tipped down over his face, and a pair of snake-skin boots.

11

She ran up to him, out of breath.

"What do I owe the honor of your visit, Miss Maxine?" he asked, tipping his Stetson and then replacing it over his wiry gray hair.

"The midwife is out at the Pruett farm, and her crusty old crow of a mother won't tell me where they live," Maxine said. "Verdie needs her; she's about to birth her baby, and I don't know what to do."

He nodded and then paused. "I know where they live," he said, removing his hat and placing it over his chest, a sullen look momentarily clouding his eyes. "I've had to take many a small pine box out to that poor old woman to bury her babies. I sure hope this one lives."

Maxine paused long enough to feel sorry for the woman even though she didn't know her.

"Can you take me and Verdie out there?"

Eddie nodded. "I'll hitch up my buckboard and bring it around the alley behind the saloon," he said looking down at his drawers. "After I make myself a little more respectable."

She bit her lip to suppress a smirk at his attire and thanked him before running back toward the saloon. When she was still a block away, she could hear Verdie's screams from the open window; even the piano and rowdy laughter from drunken patrons did not drown out her cries. She ran through the swinging doors and hollered at Thatch, the bartender. "I'm going to need help to get Verdie out to Mr. Eddie's buckboard."

"Wait a minute," Thatch hollered back. "You can't leave in the middle of your shift—and if you think you're taking a bouncer with you, you better think again!"

"Then I'll take the new swamper," she said motioning to the young man in the far corner of the saloon. He put down his mop and went over to the bar.

Thatch sighed. "Fine, but I'm making you work two nights free to make up for this, Maxine!"

"I'll do it—just help me!"

Thatch turned to the swamper. "Go upstairs and help Maxine get Verdie out to the undertaker's buckboard," he told him.

Maxine was already halfway up the stairs. "Let's go, Swamper; I need you now!" she hollered over her shoulder.

The young man paused. "Her screams stopped; she ain't dead, is she?"

The bartender shooed him with his hand. "The undertaker is taking her to the midwife; she ain't dead, she's just birthing a baby. Go see what Maxine wants you to do."

The young swamper nodded and then disappeared up the stairwell.

Maxine entered the dimly-lit room she shared with Verdie, the lantern wick flickering until she turned it up enough to see. Verdie reached out to her and Maxine took her hand.

Worry creased her brow. "Where's Miss Maisy?"

"Mr. Eddie is going to take us out to a farm just outside of town; Miss Maisy is there birthing another baby."

Verdie groaned. "I don't think there's time!"

"No, Verdie, no!" Maxine squealed as she wriggled out of her muddy dress. "You *have* to wait until we get you to Miss Maisy."

If Thatch had given her the night off the way she'd asked him to, she could have gotten to the midwife earlier. But like always, the bartender threatened her job, and she knew there were plenty of young women just as desperate as she was to have a job who waited for an opportunity like this to steal it out from under her.

"I'm so sorry I wasn't here with you tonight," Maxine said as she slipped into the most conservative dress she owned; it covered her from her collarbone to her ankles.

"I understand," Verdie said with a weak voice. "Thatch would have kicked us out of here if you didn't work."

"It doesn't make me feel any less guilty for leaving you up here all night," she said. "If Thatch hadn't given me a break to check on you, I might not have known how bad off you were. Well, he can fire me for all I care; I'm getting you to the midwife!"

She poured Verdie a glass of water from the pitcher on the bureau and helped her drink it. Then she moistened the towel and mopped up Verdie's forehead. When she finished, she used the other end to wipe away the lipstick and rouge from her own face, hoping she would be presentable enough that the Pruetts would allow her into their home for the sake of Verdie's emergency.

A knock sounded at the door, and she opened it to the young swamper they'd just hired. The boy wasn't more than eighteen years old, but he towered over Maxine by more than a foot.

He kept his eyes toward the ground. "Thatch told me to help you with whatever you needed for Miss Verdie."

He was strong enough to carry Verdie to the buckboard, and she wondered if he could be spared to go with them; someone would have to get her into the house; she and Mr. Eddie together were not as strong as this young man.

"What's your name, kid?" she asked him.

"Dobie, Ma'am," he answered, still looking at the floor.

Verdie screamed, and he jumped, his eyes lifting toward her and then back to the floor again.

"Well, get in here," Maxine said, motioning to him with her arm. "I need you to carry Verdie out to Mr. Eddie's buck-board in the alley, so we can get her to the midwife."

Maxine grabbed another quilt to stretch out on the bed of the wagon, hoping it would make Verdie more comfortable on the ride over there. Dobie went over and stood next to the bed, but Verdie let out another scream, causing the poor boy to jump again.

"Well go on, Dobie; don't let her screams worry you. She's birthing, and she's supposed to sound like that."

"Yes, Ma'am; our cow bellowed something awful when she was calving."

He swallowed and bent to pick her up, scooping her tiny frame in his arms like she was a rag doll. Verdie coiled in his arms and buried her face in his chest to muffle her cries.

"Maybe we better go down the back stairs, so we don't bother the paying customers," Maxine said, trying to keep her own worries in check. Truth be told, she was probably more scared than poor Dobie. She followed him down the back stairs and out to the alley where she found Mr. Eddie waiting. He hopped down to help Dobie get Verdie situated in the back.

"How did you get here so fast?" Maxine asked.

"My team was still hitched up from taking Holler back to his place."

Holler was a good man, but he had a tendency to wander off once he had a few shots of Red-Eye whiskey in his belly, and if someone didn't take him home every Saturday night, he'd use the church bell for target practice and it rattled Reverend Ike's nerves so much he struggled through his Sunday sermon. After the first couple of times, Mr. Eddie had taken it upon himself to become Holler's personal escort once a week, and the wealthy prospector paid him handsomely for his services.

Maxine turned to Dobie once Verdie was settled in the back. "Run inside and ask Thatch if you can go with us; we'll need help getting her out of the wagon. Tell him I'll work a third day to make up for it if I have to!"

Dobie was gone before she could say another word, and back again just as she'd settled down on the wagon bed next to Verdie, who was carrying on like an alley cat.

"He said he'll take that three days free labor from you," Dobie said as he hopped up on the seat next to Mr. Eddie, and then they were on their way out of town.

Maxine put Verdie's head in her lap and cradled her while she rolled and cried out from the pains. It frightened her, making her change her mind altogether about having children of her own someday. She felt sorry for Verdie, but she was helpless to save her from the pain.

"I need Emmett," Verdie cried out for her husband.

He'd been gone for only a few weeks, and Verdie hadn't been the same since she stood in front of the courthouse and watched the hangman pull that lever. Even her momma had been gone for too many years to remember; Maxine was the closest thing she had to family, and they weren't related even though they'd known each other as well as any two sisters could.

Maxine bit back tears. "I know," was all she could say to Verdie as she smoothed back her hair. "It's alright, I promise; everything is going to be alright."

With only the moon to guide them, Mr. Eddie steered his horse down the trail. Verdie cried out every time he hit a deep rut in the trail, and he apologized over his shoulder every time. Maxine did her best to cushion her head, but there was no getting around the jostling of her midsection. If Verdie's cries were any indication of how much it pained her, Maxine worried Verdie might have the baby before they reached the midwife. More than that; Maxine feared she'd have to be the one to catch it.

"How much further?" Maxine begged Mr. Eddie.

"Just up around this bend," he said over his shoulder.

She smoothed Verdie's auburn hair that stuck to her forehead with sweat. She'd stopped screaming, her deep bellows had turned to weak whimpering. She was burning up with fever; Maxine knew nothing about birthing babies, but she didn't think you were supposed to get a fever with it. Was she ill?

"Hurry, Mr. Eddie," Maxine warned. "I think something is wrong, she's being too quiet."

As they pulled into the yard, chickens scattered from tree branches where they'd been roosting, and Maxine ducked and squealed when one of them dove toward her. She pushed at it when it tried to land inside the bed of the wagon. Mr. Eddie steered the buckboard in front of a large home with a big red barn off to the side. It was too dark to see anything other than the silhouette of the buildings. A horse whinnied from the corral and crickets chirped happily as if the farm was normally a peaceful place to live. Maxine couldn't help thinking how lucky the Pruetts were—even if they didn't know it.

Dobie hopped down from the seat in front and lifted Verdie from the wagon bed. He carried her moaning and groaning limp body up to the door on Maxine's heels. She hesitated before knocking on the door, but a man's voice from behind them startled her.

"What do you want here?" he asked, a rifle trained on them.

"We need the midwife," Maxine said, her knees wobbling.

"She's inside with my wife; you'll have to wait until she's finished."

Verdie groaned again and let out a wail.

"My friend Verdie needs help birthing her baby, and Miss Maisy's momma told us she was out here."

He raised the shotgun. "The midwife isn't neglecting my wife to tend to that girl; we've lost too many children, and this is our last hope."

Verdie went limp in Dobie's arms, her head dangling over his arm. Maxine went to her and lifted her head, relieved that she was still breathing.

She turned to Mr. Pruett. "Look, mister; Verdie and her baby are going to die if I don't get her help, so you can risk hanging for shooting us if you want to, but we're going in there so the midwife can help her."

She rushed past Dobie and opened the door to the Pruett home, and then held the door for him while he carried Verdie into a warmly-lit sitting room with the sort of furniture you'd find at the hotels in town—fancy and clean. Every chair boasted a doily on the back and armrests, a bookshelf filled with books stood on either side of a brick fireplace hearth. The glass globes of the oil lamps were dark orange or green, blown glass, trimmed with gold filigree accents. Mrs. Pruett certainly had the finer things in life, unlike her and Verdie, who had to put up with drunken men pawing all over them just to make a few pennies. She'd worked double shifts the last few weeks, trying to help support Verdie; since her husband was hanged, she wasn't much good to the customers anyway, even despite her protruding baby-belly, which didn't seem to bother any of them in the least. Now, she would have to take care of Verdie and the baby—at least until she was strong enough to go back to work.

"Miss Maisy?" Maxine called out to the midwife.

"In here," she said through a closed door. "Who is that?"

"It's me, Maxine," she said. "I brought you Verdie—she's in a bad way and needs your help."

A door off to the side opened, and Miss Maisy poked her head out. "Bring her in here, I'll have to work both at the same time, but I'll need your help."

Dobie brought her as far as the door and transferred her to Maxine's arms. "I'll be outside with the men if you need anything else." He tipped his hat and was gone before Maxine could say a word. Maisy grabbed her legs and helped support her.

"Let's put her down over here," Miss Maisy said, letting go of her so she could spread a quilt on the floor. "I wish I could offer better accommodations."

"This is just fine, isn't it Verdie?"

She didn't answer.

Groans from Mrs. Pruett startled her and Verdie didn't answer. She was breathing, but her eyes were closed—as were Mrs. Pruett's.

"Are they okay?" Maxine whispered.

Miss Maisy nodded. "Birthing wears a woman out; if they can rest in between contractions, it's best."

Maxine held Verdie's hand; she didn't know what else to do.

"Let me get Mrs. Pruett settled, and then I'll come and check on Verdie. How close are her contractions?"

Maxine looked up at her. "What do you mean?"

"Have you been timing her contractions to see how close they're coming together?" Miss Maisy asked.

Maxine shook her head. "I didn't know I was supposed to do that, but she's been groaning regularly. She stopped screaming some time ago; I suspect b'cause she's worn out like you said."

"Did her water break?"

Maxine shrugged.

"If you don't know then it probably didn't," Miss Maisy said. "It's not good to have a dry birth."

Maxine kept quiet; she had no idea what the woman was saying and didn't want her thinking she was ignorant. She supposed she was either going to learn a lot working alongside Miss Maisy, or she'd learn the same way most women learned about birthing a child—when she was giving birth for the first time.

"Maxine," Verdie cried with a weak voice.

"I'm here," she said, grappling her shaky hand.

"I need to ask you something," Verdie stammered, her breath shallow.

Maxine shushed her. "Don't try to talk; save your energy for birthing that baby."

"Promise me…" her voice trailed off and she let out a weak cry.

Maxine's heart raced faster than a runaway horse. "Miss Maisy; help Verdie. Something's wrong!"

Maisy placed a lantern on the floor near Verdie and then knelt beside her and prodded her abdomen. "The contractions are strong," she said over Mrs. Pruett's wailing. "She's weak; she should be crying out from the pains."

Maxine flashed Miss Maisy a desperate plea with her eyes and didn't like the response in the midwife's expression. Fear gripped her heart; she couldn't lose Verdie. They'd been like sisters most of their lives; growing up in saloons hadn't been an easy life for either of them, but they'd always had each other. She held fast to her hand, watching the gentle rise and fall of her chest; it was the only way she knew Verdie was still with her.

Mrs. Pruett cried out, and Maisy went to her. Maxine cringed with every scream; if that was what birthing a baby was, she wanted no part of it. But looking at Verdie, she had to wonder why she wasn't carrying on the way the older woman was; the older woman had birthed many babies, all stillborn, according to Mr. Eddie, and she was hollering something fierce.

She felt a gentle squeeze against her hand, and she smoothed back Verdie's damp hair.

"Don't push yet," Maisy said to Mrs. Pruett.

Maxine tried to tune her out as she concentrated on Verdie.

"Promise me," Verdie said with a weak voice.

Maxine tried to shush her, but she kept trying to talk.

Her lashes fluttered in the dimly-lit room. "Promise me you'll raise my baby if something happens to me."

Maxine felt her throat constrict. "Don't you talk like that, Verdie; you hear me?"

"Promise me," Verdie managed again.

Maxine bit her bottom lip, fear working its way into her heart enough to make her cry, but she bit back the tears; the fear stayed with her. "I promise," she relented. "But I don't want to hear any more of that foolish talk. You and I are going to parade that baby into the church and have a

Christening. What did you say you wanted to name it; Beatrix after your ma if it's a girl, and Emmett after his pa—to carry on his name, if it's a boy?"

She nodded, tears streaming down her cheeks. If she knew Verdie, she was thinking of her deceased husband in this time of need and was likely mourning the loss of him all over again.

Like Maxine, Verdie never knew her pa; their mommas had been best friends and raised them in the saloons together. They'd been like family; sadly, neither of them had anyone else, and she was sure it was weighing on Verdie's shoulders right now. She was probably more frightened for her baby than Maxine was about Verdie, herself. If anything happened to her, Maxine was not her legal kin, and the sheriff would probably take the child from her and place it in the orphanage if Verdie didn't make it, but she didn't have the heart to tell Verdie that now.

And so she lied to her and it weighed on her like a millstone around her neck. If she'd been a praying woman, she'd ask God to spare Verdie, but she didn't know enough about God to think he'd care about the requests of a person like her. She'd been called a sinner her entire life, and she supposed in some ways she might be, but she'd always tried her best to be kind to others, and she wondered if that had to count for something.

Miss Maisy was at her side then, and whispered to her, a comforting hand on her shoulder. "I heard what she said," Maisy said gently. "Verdie's frightened, and fear can sometimes make us think some strange things. I won't lie to you, though, she's weak; she's had a hard time carrying this little one, but I suppose her state of mind comes mostly from what she's been through. She lost her will once her husband was hanged, and I'm worried about her now because of it. I've seen this before; you need to help get her spirits up so she can live for that baby."

Maxine gulped down the worst kind of fear; she couldn't raise a child—not by herself. Since Verdie's husband had been hanged, she knew she'd be the one to carry the burden of helping her raise the child, but if the unthinkable happened, she'd have to let the child go to the orphanage even if the sheriff did let her keep it. She had no money, and no way to support a child and still be able to work in the saloons. A baby needed round the clock care; a baby would put a damper on her ability to work.

She shook the thought from her mind; Verdie was going to live, and she would take care of both of them—that's all there was to it.

Beside her, Mrs. Pruett was oblivious to hers and Verdie's presence in her home; she was pushing her child into the world, and Maxine blocked her out to concentrate on her own troubles.

She jiggled Verdie slightly. "Wake up," she said. "I need you to…"

Verdie interrupted her with a low, grunting sort of cry. Her eyes lifted toward Miss Maisy, who was busy with Mrs. Pruett.

"What should I do?" she pleaded with the woman.

"Check to see if the baby is crowning," Maisy ordered her.

"I don't understand," Maxine said, tears choking her.

"The baby's head," she said without looking up from Mrs. Pruett. "Look to see if the baby is coming out."

Maxine hesitated.

Maisy shot her a glance. "There's no time to be timid," she scolded her. "I need you to check her for me."

"I can't," Maxine protested.

"You have to, Maxine; Verdie is counting on you, and I can't help both women at the same time. I'll walk you through it."

Maxine peeked under the blanket Verdie was wrapped in; the warm glow of the lantern illuminated the blood and fluid beneath her.

"Bend her knees so you can get a better look," Maisy instructed her.

Maxine gasped but did as she was told. She'd seen a lot serving drinks in the saloon, but this was a first.

"She's bleeding, but I see the baby's head."

Verdie groaned and let out a little cry. "Promise me," she said again, looking right through Maxine; it made her shiver despite the steaming humidity in the house.

"I promise," Maxine relented. "But I don't want to have to keep that promise to you, Verdie Wade; you push this baby out and straighten up! This little one is gonna need a momma, and I ain't ready to raise a young'un."

Verdie nodded, her lashes fluttering; Maxine knew she was using every bit of strength just to stay awake.

"Push, Verdie," Miss Maisy hollered above Mrs. Pruett's screams.

Maxine cringed when she looked up and saw Miss Maisy delivering the woman's baby. It wasn't moving or crying; was that supposed to happen? Miss Maisy walked across the room, patting the infant on the back and whispering to the child, and Maxine could hear the nervous shake in her voice.

"My baby," Mrs. Pruett cried out with a weak voice. "Can I hold her?"

Verdie pushed with all her strength, and Maxine caught the wiggling baby. The infant coughed and then wailed, bringing tears of laughter to Maxine's eyes.

"It's a girl," she whispered to Verdie.

She smiled and held her arms out for her infant and Maxine placed her in the crook of her arm. Then, Verdie's expression went dark and she cried out.

"Something's wrong with Verdie, Miss Maisy; come here quick."

Maisy knelt beside her and placed Mrs. Pruett's baby at the foot of the quilt; she flashed Maxine a quick look of despair and shook her head.

Maxine's breath caught in her throat, and she bit back tears as she looked at the lifeless infant. Her gaze lifted toward Verdie, who laid there just as lifeless as Mrs. Pruett's baby. In her arm, the little girl she'd given birth to was kicking and screaming as if she knew before Maxine did that her momma was gone.

She'd only taken her eyes off her for a minute; she hadn't been able to say goodbye. Fear flooded her mind as she gazed upon the wailing baby girl that she'd promised to care for. Her mind drank in the cries coming from Mrs. Pruett who was asking to hold her crying infant.

Maxine looked at Miss Maisy, who was busy at the foot of the quilt, fussing with Verdie and all the blood.

Without much thought, Maxine lifted the little girl from Verdie's side. "I'm sorry, Verdie; please forgive me," she whispered.

Maxine stood and handed the crying baby to Mrs. Pruett, who welcomed her with cries of laughter and cooing. Maxine stood there, numb, watching the woman cradling Verdie's crying infant and soothing her at her breast. She belonged to Mrs. Pruett now.

Maxine jumped when she heard cries from a baby behind her; how had Miss Maisy revived Mrs. Pruett's baby? Fear paralyzed her, and she couldn't turn around. What had she done? She'd given away Verdie's baby, and now this woman would have two infants; Maxine would have to explain to Mrs. Pruett what happened—or take *her* baby and raise it as Verdie's.

What was she thinking?

She whipped her head around, ready to tell Miss Maisy what she'd done, but the stillborn baby still lay on the quilt at Verdie's feet. In the midwife's arms was another wailing baby.

Maxine dropped to her knees beside Miss Maisy. "What happened?"

Maisy smiled. "Verdie had another baby; she pushed her out with her last breath." She wrapped the infant in the small quilt Verdie had brought with her and then handed the healthy baby girl to Maxine. Tears made her lower lip quiver as she held the baby close to her.

"I gave that one to Mrs. Pruett," she whispered. "Can I let her keep it? I can't take care of two."

"Verdie bequeathed her baby—babies to you, so you have the authority to do with them as you see fit," Maisy whispered.

"What about that one?" she asked Miss Maisy pointing to the stillborn.

"I'm going to have to tell her husband the truth; he'll have to decide what to do."

Miss Maisy pulled the quilt over Verdie's face and then wrapped the stillborn baby in the small quilt beneath her. Maxine's breath hitched, and she bit down tears as she cradled the other baby in her arms. Verdie had twins; was she going to have to take both of them, or would the Pruett's agree to raise the other one? She looked back at Mrs. Pruett who was happily cooing the child she thought was hers; there was no way she was going to get Verdie's child away from her now, and Maxine was content with that.

Miss Maisy carried the stillborn infant out of the room, careful to keep it hidden from Mrs. Pruett. Maxine followed her out to the kitchen where the menfolk had gathered.

Mr. Pruett rose from his chair, his eyes trained on the lifeless bundle in the midwife's arms. His breath hitched as his gaze turned to the wiggly infant in Maxine's arms and then back to the stillborn he knew was his child. He withheld tears as he reached out for his child.

"What is it?" he asked, his voice cracking.

"It's a girl," the midwife answered.

"Did you have to give her something to make her sleep—like the last time?" he asked.

The midwife shook her head. "She's awake."

"I must go to her," he said, handing back the infant without lifting the quilt to look at it.

Miss Maisy held back from taking the infant from him. "There's something you should know before you go in there."

Alarm consumed his face. "Is she…?"

Miss Maisy shook her head. "I told you; your wife is awake, and quite content."

He pointed to the bundle in the midwife's arms. "She doesn't know?"

"It's my fault," Maxine blurted out.

Mr. Pruett's face twisted up with anger, his eyes narrowing and his cheeks heating. "What did you do?"

"My friend, Verdie, had twins and I gave one of the girls to your wife; she thinks the baby is hers."

"She must know the truth!" he said through gritted teeth.

He pushed past the two women and barged into the room where his wife was so content with the infant in her arms, she was unaware of Verdie lying dead on the floor in the room.

Mr. Eddie came in from outside where he'd probably been out smoking a cigar and Maxine rushed to him, her lower lip quivering. "Verdie didn't make it!"

"Where is she?"

Maxine burst into tears. "She's in the bedroom wrapped in a quilt."

He looked at the bundle in the midwife's arms and reached for it. "I guess we will have *two* burials?"

Miss Maisy nodded, tears streaming down her cheeks.

Mr. Eddie and Dobie took the Pruett baby out to the buckboard while the women waited for Mr. Pruett to return from talking to his wife.

After a few minutes, he returned to the kitchen, his face ashen, his eyes red-rimmed.

"Does she want to keep the baby?" Miss Maisy asked gently. "I have to know so it can be recorded."

He slumped into the nearest chair, his expression blank. "I haven't seen my wife this happy in many years. The child we were expecting—the doctor told us before he left that it was our last chance. She will never be able to have another child. She was so happy I didn't have the heart to tell her it wasn't our child—she believes it is ours."

He flashed a worried glance toward the gurgling infant in Maxine's arms. "You *gave* her the child?"

Maxine nodded. "I didn't know there was going to be two of them. Before Verdie died, she made me promise I would raise her child if something happened to her. I agreed."

His attention turned to the midwife. "You are witness to this conversation and will swear to it?"

"Yes, Mr. Pruett," she answered.

He jumped from the chair and went to the counter and reached above the cupboard for a coffee can and brought it down. He emptied the contents out onto the table and scrambled to pick up the coins and paper notes. Then he shoved it toward Maxine, urging her to take it.

"It's more than a hundred dollars," he said, desperation in his tone. "Take it and go somewhere else with the other child—far from here. She must never know there is another child that bears the same face, or she'll know her own child was stillborn. She can't handle another death. But if you stay here and raise the twin, it will break her."

Maxine had always wanted to go to San Francisco; a hundred dollars would give her and the baby a fresh new start. She hadn't wanted to raise Verdie's child because she worried it would be a hardship, but with the Pruett's money, it didn't have to be.

She nodded, and he stuffed the money back into the coffee can and handed it to her. "Thank you!" he said, forcing a smile.

She nodded again.

Mr. Pruett's mood changed. "I would appreciate you leaving town after your friend's funeral," he said firmly. "It's not that I'm not grateful for what your friend gave up for us, but I need it to be this way; I hope you understand."

"I have one condition," Maxine said. "You must name the child Beatrix; it was the name Verdie picked out."

He nodded, and Maxine left, thinking it was going to be a long and sad ride back into town sitting in the back of the buckboard beside two dead bodies.

# TWO

*Tombstone, Arizona Territory, Autumn, 1885*

*Twenty-one years later…*

Beatrix Pruett stepped off the stage and onto the boardwalk in the dusty town of Tombstone. She slapped at the skirt of her navy traveling dress, sending clouds of dust rolling off the fabric, where it lingered in the stagnant heat. Though she was happy to be free from the constant jostling of the rattling stagecoach, the air outside the coach was not much cooler. A bead of sweat rolled behind her corset, causing her to wriggle beneath the confinement of the garment. She'd scarcely been able to breathe for the duration of her ride from the train depot in Benson. The train had been rather crowded, and though she'd longed to recline in one of the private booths, the Superintendent of the school board had sent her a general boarding pass for the train marked *Coach*.

She arched her back, stretching her sore muscles and rolling her stiff neck while the stage driver tossed her bag and her trunk onto the boardwalk. She stood beside them, waiting for the promised escort from Mr. Wallaby from the school board, but she didn't see anyone fitting the description of a schoolmaster.

Though it was the middle of the afternoon, the streets bustled with carriages, passersby and a loudness she didn't care for. Why hadn't Mr. Wallaby warned her of the rowdiness of this town when he'd offered her the position as the school teacher? She was nervous enough with this being her first teaching position since she'd earned her certificate, but to stand alone on the boardwalk without an escort filled her with a measure of fear that compared only to what she'd felt the night her momma had died.

A fast tune played from a piano not far from her, and she slighted her eyes to glance at the sign above the swinging door of the Silver Dollar Saloon only a few feet from her that boasted dancing girls and gambling. Roars of laughter from men and squeals from women made her cringe more than the tang of stale whiskey that floated on the dry and dusty heat wave migrating through the street. Women weren't allowed in the saloons unless they worked there, and she'd heard stories about the *soiled doves* from Reverend Ike's sermons back home in El Paso, but she failed to believe those women were as happy as they sounded.

*Thank you, Lord, that you spared me from such a life. Bless the soiled doves in the saloon and send help to open their eyes to your truth before it's too late for them.*

Standing there alone, she wished her daddy had been able to travel with her, but she was due to begin teaching on Monday; he'd insisted she take his Derringer along and it weighed down her reticule on her wrist like a millstone. She may as well have traveled with a large rock, for all the good a handgun she had no intention of using would do her, while her real protector, her father, stayed behind in El Paso and wouldn't be able to visit her until after he'd settled a few financial matters.

The clinking of spurs against the boardwalk from behind caused her to turn her head. As he approached her, his tin star gleamed in the sunlight, momentarily blinding her, but his swagger and smile hypnotized her. He wore his gun low like a gun fighter, and the set of his jaw was rugged enough to intimidate even the wildest of outlaws, yet swoon-worthy enough to wrangle any woman. Beatrix could no more take her eyes off the sheriff than she could stand clear of his path so he wouldn't run smack into her when he reached the very spot where she stood.

Luckily for her, he stopped just short and tipped his Stetson from his dark hair as he extended his hand to her.

"I meant to be here in time to meet the stage," he said, his low, smoky baritone making her knees feel wobbly. He brought her hand to his full lips and kissed the back, his moustache tickling through her thin gloves.

She bit her bottom lip to suppress a giggle.

"I'm Sheriff Muley Ransome; the Superintendent of the school board, Mr. Wallaby, couldn't be here to meet the early stage because school hasn't let out just yet."

Her parasol dropped against her shoulder, startling her enough to manage a nod and a weak smile, but she was unable to find her voice.

"You must be Miss Beatrix Pruett; I've heard so much about you," he said, his blue eyes reaching deep into her soul and tugging at her heartstrings.

She tightened her grip on her parasol and cleared her throat. She was not here to swoon over the sheriff; her teaching contract would forbid her to marry for two years, and it would be a long two years if she were to let her mind wander in that direction. Besides, her logical side reminded her, he'd merely greeted her; never mind her immediate need to collapse into his capable arms where she would feel safe.

"I'm pleased to make your acquaintance, Sheriff," she squeaked out, trying to hide the terror she felt about being alone in the rowdy town.

"I could walk you down to the boarding house if you'd like an escort," he said with a smile and a tip of his hat over his thick, wavy brown hair. "Mrs. Hopkins has your room reservation through the weekend."

She paused, forgetting her manners; his smiling blue eyes had her so hypnotized she almost didn't catch what he said about her room.

"Why did Mr. Wallaby reserve my room for only a few days?" she asked, worry in her tone.

The sheriff chuckled. "It's customary for the bride to move in with her husband after the wedding."

"Wedding?" she squealed, and then put a hand over her mouth, pausing to assure a more ladylike tone. "I'm not getting married."

"That's why the Schoolmaster sent for you," the sheriff said. "He's told everyone in town you're his mail-order bride."

Beatrix sucked in her breath. "I am no such thing! The nerve of that man luring me out here to this wilderness on the pretense of taking the position of school teacher, only to…oh no!"

"He's the Schoolmaster, Miss Pruett," the sheriff interrupted her. "There isn't another school where you can teach."

"I demand you press charges against Mr. Wallaby for fraud! He's soiling my good name and my pa will be so ashamed when he comes to visit me. You have to undo this for me!"

"I can't do that, Miss; he showed me your signature on the marriage contract himself."

"He sent me a teaching contract—not a marriage contract," Beatrix insisted.

She flipped her lace fan and began to swish it in front of her face, but it did her no good; tears welled up from her throat and she bit them back.

"Maybe you should wait and discuss this with Mr. Wallaby," the sheriff suggested. "Maybe it's all just a big misunderstanding."

Beatrix lifted her chin. "There is nothing to discuss; I'm not in the habit of agreeing to marrying a stranger, much less, a man I don't love! I would never enter into a contract for marriage as a mail-order bride; I assure you I signed a teaching contract and nothing more. I traveled here on the promise that I was to be the new school teacher. You have to believe me."

"I'm sorry, Miss Pruett, but we already have a school teacher and he needs a bride—which is why he sent away for you."

"I wasn't *sent* for like cattle!" she cried.

She fumbled with her reticule and pulled out her teaching certificate and showed it to Sheriff Muley.

"I'm sorry, but this does me no good. I already told you we have a teacher. If you can't prove to me you're not a mail-order bride, then, as the sheriff, I'm going to have to hold you to your contract to marry Mr. Wallaby."

"No!" she cried. "I can't get married to a man I don't love; please don't make me!"

"Why don't we wait until we talk to Mr. Wallaby."

"No!" she squealed. "I don't want to see him; I have to leave." She turned back to the stage driver, who was waiting on his new passengers. "Driver, please put my trunk back on the stage; I have to get out of here."

Sheriff Muley put his hand on her arm and gently nudged her. "I'm afraid I can't let you get on that stage—not until we clear this up. I'm going to need to see the contract again."

"I don't have the papers I signed; I sent them back to the schoolmaster," she said, sobbing. "Please let me go; I need to go home."

"I'm afraid I can't let you do that," Sheriff Muley said. "Not until we have a look at that contract."

Beatrix put a hand to her chest and gasped.

"I can't breathe!" she cried.

Sheriff Muley put his arm around her to steady her, but she collapsed against his strong frame and everything went black.

Sheriff Muley wrapped his arms around Miss Pruett in time to keep her from falling onto the boardwalk. Scooping her up into his arms, she let out a little sigh and went limp in his arms like a rag doll.

He hollered up to the stage driver to get someone to take her things to the boarding house. Shifting her in his arms, her hat came loose from her silky auburn tendrils and tumbled to his feet.

As he rested her against him, he couldn't help but breathe her in; the slightest hint of lemon verbena radiated from her skin.

*How could the school master be so lucky to get a woman like her for a mail-order bride?*

Muley let out a discouraging breath; unless she was telling the truth about the contract she'd signed, he needed to keep his mind on getting her to the doctor. He was sworn to uphold the law, even if that meant turning such an angel over to the schoolmaster.

He shuddered at the thought of her being in Mr. Wallaby's arms; the man was probably twice her age.

If only she didn't smell so wonderful and feel so sweet in his arms. He felt sorry for her; she clearly did not want to marry Mr. Wallaby, and Muley had a hunch that once she met the older man, she'd feel even more strongly against the idea of being forced into a marriage with him.

She nuzzled his neck as he walked into the doctor's office, and his mind began to reel with ideas on how to get her out of the mess she was in with the schoolmaster.

# THREE

BEATRIX awoke to the strong odor of smelling salts beneath her nose. She coughed and turned her head away from the smell, a woozy feeling overtaking her. She lurched upright on the settee, feeling disoriented and too warm, a faint memory of being in the arms of the sheriff haunting her.

Had she *kissed* him?

She drew in a gasping breath and brought her hand to the bodice of her dress and patted; it was still there. Relief flooded her as she let her gaze scan the dimly-lit room, an oil lamp flickering the scene in and out and she was aware of someone else in the room—the sheriff, perhaps?

She pointed to the lamp. "Turn up the wick! I can't see!"

An older gentleman with white hair and wire-rimmed spectacles reached for the brass wheel on the side of the lamp and turned it until the room was illuminated. She threw her legs over the side of the settee and planted them on the wood floor, scanning the many cabinets filled with medicine bottles and medical instruments she had no idea what they were used for. Two certificates graced the far wall above a small desk that sat askew in the corner of the room. She was in a doctor's office—but where?

"Welcome back, young lady," the man said. "I'm Doctor Haywood."

He went to the stand beside the exam table and poured a glass of water from the pitcher and handed it to her. She sipped slowly, trying to keep her head from fogging again. It suddenly hit her where she was, and she sprang to her feet.

"I have to get out of here," she said. "Where's my reticule and my trunk?"

The doctor retrieved her reticule from a hook behind the door and handed it to her. "I don't think you should leave until you've gotten your bearings. I'd hate to have you faint again out on the street."

Everything was slowly coming back to her; she'd fainted, and the sheriff had caught her. She scanned the room, noting he wasn't there now. Perhaps if she left quickly, she could escape him and leave town before he tried to force her to meet with the devious Mr. Wallaby.

Noticing her reticule wasn't as heavy as it had been, Beatrix stuffed her hand inside and felt around. Her fingers met with her teaching certificate and a few other papers, her mother's locket, her handkerchief, and a bottle of lemon verbena, but nothing else. Her father's Derringer was missing.

A quick knock at the door startled her, but her blood pooled in her feet when the sheriff entered the room, making her feel as if they were nailed to the floor. She wanted to flee, but she was paralyzed with fear.

"I'm glad to see you're alright," Sheriff Muley said. "I've sent for Mr. Wallaby, so we can clear up the confusion about why you're here."

"No!" she squealed.

The sheriff furrowed his brows impatiently.

"If Mr. Wallaby clears you of the contract as his mail-order bride, then you're free to go."

"Why does he get to decide?" she asked. "Don't you believe me?"

She stared into his blue eyes, finding a hint of regret in them. Was it possible he was on *her* side? If he was, she could use that to her advantage. Though Beatrix didn't have a devious bone in her body, her freedom and her future were at stake, and she was not about to give up either of them to a man who was trying to trick her.

She studied the sheriff, her face flushing with anxiety. "Where's my father's Derringer?"

"A woman in your state of mind shouldn't be concealing such a weapon. It's in my office in the gun safe. You can have it back when we sort out the misunderstanding with Mr. Wallaby."

"You have no right to take my only form of protection!" she said, her voice shaky. "I haven't broken the law; your schoolmaster has!"

"No one said you broke the law, and I haven't seen any evidence that Mr. Wallaby has either. I understand you're upset, and you might have reason to be, but as the sheriff, it's my duty to uphold the law in this town. If I have suspicion you might lose control of your emotions and be tempted to use that Derringer on a certain schoolmaster because you think he tricked you in some way—and he may have—then I think it's best if I hang on to that weapon until we sort this out."

"And just how do you expect me to defend myself in this rowdy town without a proper escort or the use of my Derringer?" she asked.

"I'll be more than happy to escort you around town," Sheriff Muley said. "That is, until your betrothed takes over."

"That man is *not* my betrothed!"

Another knock on the door startled Beatrix and she stepped behind the sheriff as an older gentleman entered the office. His clothing was tailored, but it was tattered and in need of mending. He removed his hat revealing a balding head, a ring of wiry gray hair tufted in an unruly manner. He lifted a pocket-watch from his vest pocket and glanced at the face. "I would have been here sooner, but I had to talk to Mr. Barney again about his oldest."

Mr. Wallaby stepped forward with an air of arrogance and presented a contract to the sheriff for him to examine. "Is that not a contract for marriage?" he asked.

The sheriff held the contract and Beatrix peered over his shoulder at her signature at the bottom of the page. "That is a teaching contract," she said. "It says so right at the top of the page!"

"Yes, indeed," Mr. Wallaby said. "But if you read a little further down the page, it clearly states in the context of the contract that the only capacity in which you will teach is at my side—as my wife, and only as my assistant."

Beatrix twisted her face in anger. "You tricked me!"

"And you obviously did not read the contract before you signed, but that still does not relieve you from the obligation."

"That contract had to have been written by a lawyer," she said, scowling at the man. "I had to stop reading after the third paragraph because I didn't understand the rest of it. I never dreamed you would have a legal contract written by a lawyer with wording that committed me something I would have never agreed to if I'd understood it."

"Yes, indeed, I did have the best lawyer in town draw up the contract, and it contains a clause that states that your signature binds you to marry me in order to take the teaching position."

"Then I won't take the teaching position!" she squealed.

"Then you will be in breach of contract and I will have to press charges against you."

Beatrix turned to the sheriff. "He can't do that, can he?"

"I'm afraid he can," Sheriff Muley said in a tone that reflected defeat. "So unless you can prove this isn't your signature, you're betrothed to Mr. Wallaby."

Beatrix looped her arm in the sheriff's and jutted out her chin toward Mr. Wallaby. "The sheriff compromised me when you were not here to meet me at the stage; I believe that makes me *his* betrothed!"

Sheriff Muley wagged his finger at her. "Now, we both know that isn't true, Miss Pruett. I am not in the habit of compromising another man's betrothed—or *any* woman, for that matter!"

She raised her chin a little higher. "Are you denying I was in your arms, Sheriff?"

His gaze bore a hole right through her and went straight to her pleading heart, and she could see by the smirk he tried hard to suppress beneath his moustache that he had caught on to what she was trying to accomplish.

"No, I won't deny that," he admitted.

She flashed him smiling eyes and he reciprocated by turning his head toward her and winking at her.

"Do you also deny that I kissed you?"

"That's also true," he said. "You did kiss me."

Her heart thumped; she hadn't dreamed it!

Mr. Wallaby wagged a finger at the two of them. "I won't tolerate this!" he hollered. "I'll press charges against both of you if Miss Pruett isn't in front of the preacher to marry me after the service on Sunday!"

# FOUR

Trixie Donovan stepped off the afternoon stage onto the boardwalk in Tombstone and breathed in the stench of the city. It wasn't as pungent as the Barbary Coast had been, but it possessed the same general air of manure in the streets and back-alley privies. The only thing missing was the melody of seagulls and buoy bells at the wharf, and the scent of drunken men sleeping off Shanghai Pete's catch of the day aboard the departing vessels at the docks.

She adjusted her low-cut, red dress, pulling the thin straps down over her shoulders and yanked on the bottom of the skirt that was nearly short enough to show her scandalously short bloomers. Her auburn hair cascaded over her bare shoulders, falling beneath the Stetson she'd purposely stained a deep pink using crushed berries so that it would match her dress. Her feet were clad in calf-length, pointed-toe, riding boots made from the finest leather; her spurs clanked across the boardwalk as she strolled down the block, peering in all the windows of the many shops in town. She liked wearing spurs on her boots; it drew attention to her, and that was good for business. With her six-guns strapped to her narrow waist, she was ready to go looking for work.

Her first stop would be the biggest saloon in town, and she would work her way down to the smaller ones if she were rejected at the first one. She didn't worry about that; her momma had taught her well by example when it came to landing a job at the saloon.

Trixie's momma, Maxine, had passed away when she was only fifteen, leaving her to fend for herself. Despite the promise she'd made to the woman to never step foot in a saloon, she'd broken that promise when merchants refused her respectable work after learning she was Maxine's daughter, and they'd branded her a soiled dove before giving her a chance to live a reputable life.

She'd watched her momma try many times during her childhood to gain proper employment in whatever town they ended up in, but every time she'd find work that allowed her to hold her head up, she always ended up back in the saloon. The good jobs never lasted more than a few days and it would always end the same way. She'd been a seamstress, a hotel maid, and even a dishwasher for several restaurants. But there was always a cowhand or a miner who knew her past as a barmaid in the saloons, and they would expose her past to her current employer. Then, she would immediately be let go from her job, and she would end up right back in the saloon looking for work again. No matter where they went, it was always the same. It had been her momma's dream to live in California, and when they finally made it there when she was ten years old, they ended up at the Barbary coast and her momma gave up trying to find proper jobs and headed straight for the many saloons to look for work.

It had been a hard life for her momma, and now, that life had trickled down to her.

That is until the day Wild Willy Wilcox had introduced himself to Trixie a couple of weeks ago. He talked fast and drank a lot, but he had big dreams of getting money the easy way, and Trixie wanted in on his plan the moment he invited her to share a cut of the profit.

Wild Willy had given Trixie hope that she could put her saloon days behind her just as soon as they hit *pay dirt,* as he referred to his biggest scheme ever—robbing the Wells Fargo stagecoach of the miners' payroll. He'd filled Trixie's head with dreams of living on her own in a nice house in town and having the fanciest of clothes to wear that all the women would envy, and it would make them respect her instead of looking down their noses at her when they passed her in the street.

Her arrival in Tombstone meant the last saloon job Trixie would ever have to take; six years in the saloons was too much for the young girl who felt her youth slipping away from her just as it had for her momma.

This saloon job was only as a cover to get information. Trixie told herself that robbing the miners' payroll was simply a faster way to part them from their money rather than getting it in small pittances when they drank it away in the saloon. Wild Willy had convinced her that taking from them in one large sum was beneficial to both parties. By taking the money before they had a chance to squander it, the miners would be spared the guilt they lived with on a daily basis having to face the truth that their drunkenness and carousing was hurting their families. As for Trixie, she would benefit by not having to waste the rest of her life serving them those drinks in a filthy saloon. This would allow her the chance to live the good life while she was still young enough to enjoy it. Watching her momma die from the weakness of living a hard life, she was not too eager to follow in the woman's footsteps, but would rather be free from the life of a soiled dove.

Trixie pushed through the swinging doors of the Silver Dollar Saloon, her spurs clinking against the floor immediately drew the attention of the bartender in her direction. It was early, and the place had not yet filled to capacity. In the corner, the swamper swished his rag mop against the roughly-hewn floorboards, making a muddy mess of the dirt caked on the floors. Trixie knew it would take him all night to mop the floors, but they would never be fully clean.

She smiled her best smile and winked at the large man behind the bar as she sauntered closer. It roiled her stomach to act in such a way, but she was desperate to pull this off one last time before she was free. Her freedom from this life meant everything to her; she'd promised her momma on her deathbed that she would never resort to working saloons, and she'd regretted breaking that promise. She would soon make her momma proud by leaving this life behind.

*Only a few more days and I'll be free;* she reminded herself.

Trixie made her way to the bar; the older man behind the counter hadn't broken eye contact with her since she'd entered the smoky room despite the many heated discussions in progress over card games that filled the large establishment.

Trixie smiled with confidence when she approached the bar, the very large barkeep smiling around the cigar clenched between rotted teeth. She suppressed a wave of disgust that swept over her, keeping her smile from fading.

The barman removed the cigar from his teeth and pinched it between his thumb and index finger, holding it in mid-air while he inspected her from head-to-toe. "You must be new in town," the barman said, licking his lips and raising wiry brows over bulging eyes. "You looking for work, Miss?"

"I don't need to look," she said with a confidence that would have her momma turning in her grave. "I've found it!"

"It pays room and board," he said. "You keep the tips, but you have to provide your own dresses—especially if you have more like the one you're wearing." He sounded positively charmed by the act she'd put on just for the occasion, and that amused Trixie.

He reached out and ran a finger down her arm, and she jerked away, lifting her six-guns from their holsters with one quick motion; she shoved one in his belly and pushed the other up under his chin, drawing back on the hammers just before they made contact with the bartender.

Taking him by surprise, he threw up his hands.

She gritted her teeth at him. "No one touches me; understood?"

"As you wish, Miss—uh—what should I call you?" he asked, his voice a little shaky.

If there was one thing her momma had left her with, it was to put fear in any man before letting him see how scared she was. She could only shoot with one hand, but he didn't need to know that; she held them both in place with confidence.

"The name's Trixie," she said with a grin. "I'm a sharp-shooter, so pass the word around; I'll shoot first and ask questions later, and I sleep with my guns. You'll be smart to remember that!"

He attempted to nod with her gun still pushing his chin up as far as she could reach.

She could see in his eyes that he'd made a mental note; *crazy girl with guns!*

She was okay with that.

He swallowed hard. "There's a vacant room upstairs at the end of the hall; the first set of clean linens are provided, but you'll be responsible for washing them as long as you occupy the room."

She lowered her guns and holstered them and then went back toward the door. "I need someone to get my trunk; I left it at the ticket office for the stage."

The swamper stood at the end of the bar and shook his head.

The bartender leered at him. "You got something to say, Swamper?"

"Why'd you give her a job?" he asked in a low tone.

The bartender chuckled. "I'm feeling charitable today. Besides, she's too pretty to let go to the competition."

"She's probably more trouble than she's worth," he said, keeping his voice low.

"You fetch her trunk in a hurry and be back here to finish mopping up the floors, and let me worry about the entertainment around here," the old man scolded him.

Trixie slowly descended from the upper floor, making certain her spurs clinked on each wooden step, purposely drawing attention to herself. As planned, all eyes gapcd up at her as she made her way down to the barroom floor. She'd succeeded in making an entrance; now, with all eyes in the room on her, she nodded to the man at the piano and belted out a song as she descended the stairwell. Roars of applause and hollers of praise came from the crowd of men in the room, whistles abounding. This pleased Trixie, who knew that winning over a room full of drunken men would mean they would soon part with their money, and it would belong to her.

When she finished her song, every man in the room invited her to sit with him, much to the chagrin of the other women who worked there. From them, she received scowls, and she preferred that. It kept her from having to make friends with any of them, and that would keep her from being riddled with guilt for the business she was stealing from them by being the center of attention.

"Gentlemen," she said with a smile. "There is enough of me to go around; I plan on getting to know every one of you before the night is over!"

They all cheered as they nudged one another to be the first to buy her a drink.

In the corner, the other women gathered and whispered. Trixie had a hunch they were plotting to get her fired, but she didn't plan to stay there long enough to give them a chance to follow through with any plans they may be concocting against her.

She only cared about one thing; finding out what day the Wells Fargo stagecoach delivered the payroll and where it was divvied out to the miners.

# FIVE

Beatrix went to the parlor when Miss Mavis, the boarding house owner, called her downstairs for her *date* with the sheriff. She'd worn her Sunday best dress, and she hoped he would approve; judging by the look of surprise in his eyes, she'd say he did. He'd put on a fresh shirt and combed his dark, sandy hair to the side. He clenched his hat between his white-knuckled fingers, and he held it in front of his chest. The tin star on his lapel sparkled as if he'd shined it, and his boots were cleaner than she'd seen them earlier that day. He was a handsome man, his blue eyes gleaming at her as she entered the room. It made her hope more than ever that their plan to be seen in public would discourage Mr. Wallaby from pursuing the lawsuit against her. She knew that Sheriff Muley was merely humoring her and had done her a public service by protecting her from the trickery of the schoolmaster and hoping he could expose him for the fraud he was. But it did more than that for her; it made her wish that she could explore her attraction to the sheriff just a bit more. She prayed there would be plenty of time for that later; for now, she had to get back her freedom the overbearing older man was threatening to take from her.

Sheriff Muley held out his arm to her. "Are you ready to go to supper?" he asked. "I took the liberty of making an inquiry at the Palace Restaurant on the way over here, and they're keeping their best table for us."

She looped her arm in his and smiled. "That sounds delightful."

He escorted her outside into the early evening. Though he still had not returned her father's Derringer, she felt safer than she thought possible on the arm of the Sheriff. If nothing else, she would enjoy the evening and take the time to learn more about her dinner companion. Surely, her father would not object to her having a meal with a man of the law. She was certain, however, that her father would strongly object to her marrying Mr. Wallaby. But would he object to her marrying the sheriff? She felt confident that her father would give his blessing for that union, but she doubted it would come to such a drastic end. After all, she and the sheriff were merely pretending to be betrothed; it was doubtful they would have to actually marry to be rid of Mr. Wallaby.

They strolled along the boardwalk to the end of the block where the Palace Restaurant and Hotel stood majestically among the other businesses surrounding it. The building itself was grander than anything Beatrix had seen in El Paso, which was nothing more than a small cow-town.

They entered the restaurant, making certain that prominent townsfolk saw them together in a proper setting. The lavish lobby of the building showed off a round, red velvet settee in the center of the room, where the sheriff left her to speak with the maître d' who stood sentry duty at the hand-carved podium in the wide doorway that separated the restaurant from the hotel staircase.

As they entered the dining room, all conversations turned to gasps and whispers, the clanking of dishes rising above the hushed crowd in the room. All eyes were upon them, and it made Beatrix tighten her grip on the Sheriff's arm.

They were seated in the middle of the dining room, and she wondered if they should have thought this through a little better before deciding on such a conspicuous table. It was too late; all she could do was to force a smile to all who ogled her, their eyes scrutinizing her as if to examine her worthiness to be in the company of their sheriff.

He seated her and then sat across from her, the waiter already standing at attention with a tray containing a water pitcher and two glasses. He set the glasses down and poured without a word, and then replaced the pitcher and handed them both a couple of menus.

"Do you like sweet tea?" the sheriff asked Beatrix.

She nodded shyly, and he ordered two glasses from the waiter. She hadn't been to such a fancy restaurant before, and she had no idea how to act. She would use her best table manners; Momma had taught her the importance of manners and how they would play a part in landing a husband someday. Little had she known that her signature on the wrong piece of paper would supersede all the lessons her momma had bestowed upon her. She'd been so excited to receive her first teaching invitation that she hadn't bothered to read the entire, difficult to understand contract, and now she wished she had. Pride had played a part in keeping her from asking the advice of her father, and thinking back, she regretted not seeking his wise counsel about the contract she signed.

Now that she was seated across from the handsome sheriff with his intoxicating smile, she feared Mr. Wallaby would never release her from the contract. Her father would arrive in Tombstone at the end of the week, and he would be disappointed in her carelessness if she could not find a way to fix this. She was desperate, to say the least, and if using the sheriff to get her out of the jam would work, she would sit in this uncomfortable dining room, and she would smile for all who stared.

She sipped her tea and fumbled with her glass, nearly spilling the tea when she replaced it on the table. Perhaps it was best to keep her hands in her lap until she could get used to the awkwardness of being here. Surely, it was better for her to sit here with the sheriff than to be seated across from Mr. Wallaby as his wife.

Would the man be able to afford such a place on his teaching salary? And what of the sheriff? Was he given such rights of passage into the finest of establishments in exchange for his protection of the community, or had he spent an entire month's wages on this evening? She looked over the menu, deciding if he had to pay for the dinner, she would order the least expensive item, and that was the baked chicken.

He looked up from his menu and smiled. "Order whatever you like," he said, leaning in a little closer to whisper. "I get one free meal every week here, and I haven't used my last two, so tonight is *on the house!"*

*What a relief because I'm hungry enough to eat the thickest steak on the menu!*

She smiled. "Thank you; I was thinking how hungry I am after that long ride on the stage. We stopped at the way station, but my stomach was so upset from all the jostling, I neglected to eat anything."

"It's a rough ride," he agreed. "Especially for a lady."

She nodded. "Even in my most comfortable traveling dress, I was miserable."

She knew they were making small talk and it didn't bother her as much as the silence and the stares from the other patrons.

He leaned in a little further and whispered again. "Maybe we should discuss our plans to marry so everyone will overhear."

Her heart thumped a little harder, but she had to admit this was pretty exciting. It sure beat watching the cattle grazing back in Texas. She nodded to him, and he cleared his throat as he leaned back in his chair.

"Have you decided on what you'll eat, my darling?" he asked a little louder than she'd wanted him to.

She felt heat rising in her cheeks as she glanced up at him, noting the gleam in his eyes.

He was enjoying this!

"I can't decide, darling," she said, trying not to laugh. "Perhaps you could choose for me."

The waiter returned and took their menus.

Sheriff Muley looked up at the waiter. "We'll both have a steak and baked potato with green beans."

"Excellent choice, Sheriff," the waiter said. "I'll be back in a minute with some fresh bread for the table."

"Thank you," the sheriff said, and then waved to the violin player to come over to their table to serenade Beatrix. Her cheeks heated again as the man played a soulful tune, but she was enjoying the attention. She'd never had a beau before; she'd dated a few boys back home, but she'd never had a date like this. She sat up a little taller in her chair; the sheriff was doing his best to make her feel special, and his efforts would not be wasted on her.

As the music played, she allowed her mind to wander to her dinner companion. She was curious about why Sheriff Muley didn't have a wife or even a girlfriend. So far, he'd been the perfect gentleman, and he was the most handsome man in the room; or maybe it was that she already had eyes only for him.

Sheriff Muley reached across the table for her hands, and she placed hers in his. They were warm and inviting and made her skin tingle all the way to her elbows. Was it proper to hold hands in public? She didn't care; to Beatrix, she and the sheriff felt like the only two people in the room.

How far would he take this act? Would they actually marry? The whole idea thrilled her. The musician finished, and Sheriff Muley pulled a coin from his pocket and tipped the man before he left their table.

Sheriff leaned close to her again. "I think we should talk to a lawyer tomorrow—just to see if he can do anything to get you out of that contract."

"Certainly not the same one who wrote that contract for Mr. Wallaby!"

He squeezed her hands affectionately. "Don't you worry, my dear; we'll talk to a friend of mine, Charles Bodine."

Why was he still speaking to her so affectionately? Was his reason in case the tables around them should overhear him? Whatever the reason, she liked it; she could get used to this.

For the remainder of the evening, Sheriff Muley entertained her with one story after another. She'd never laughed so much in all her life. He was certainly an interesting man. She'd shared a few stories of her own, and surprisingly, he laughed at her stories too, and that pleased her. It was refreshing to Beatrix that they shared so much joy in laughter. Her momma had always told Beatrix that if she could find a man who could make her laugh the same way her father made her momma laugh that she should marry him.

Surely, there was never a better sign than that.

At the end of the evening, he'd held her hand on the walk home. The moonlight shone brightly on the boardwalk, and the stars twinkled up above them. It tickled her heart that he'd made her feel just like one of the stars twinkling in the night sky.

When they reached the boardinghouse at the end of the block, the lantern was lit in the front parlor; Miss Mavis was waiting up for her.

Sheriff Muley stopped her before they walked up the stone path that led to the porch.

"I'd like to have lunch with you at the hotel before we see Charles if that suits you," he said. "Do you think I can come by and pick you up at noon?"

"Yes, I'd like that," she said.

He smiled, and it made her knees wobble. Then he leaned in and kissed her cheek gently; his lips lingered only long enough to send shivers through her that shot right to her toes.

"Good night," the sheriff said.

"Thank you for dinner," she said. "Good night."

He walked her up to the porch and kissed her cheek once more. She suppressed the urge to kiss him back, knowing that to do so would mean they were truly engaged, and she had to remind herself their relationship wasn't real.

# SIX

TRIXIE finished another song just as the door swung open and Wild Willy entered the bar. He ignored her and went straight to the bar and ordered a shot of Red Eye whiskey. He turned around and lifted the shot glass of the deep amber liquid, saluted Trixie, and then tipped his head back, swallowing it in one gulp.

In turn, she ignored him, as he had instructed her earlier that day at the hotel, where they'd met briefly to go over his plan. She'd already overheard enough conversations in the saloon to know which one of the miners was drunk enough to tell her the details of the payroll. Now that she'd finished her song, she intended to sit in on the poker game in progress where her pigeon and his friends were enjoying a friendly game with a couple of cowpokes.

She walked over and draped her arms around the back of the youngest miner at the table and tried not to gag. He smelled as if he hadn't had a bath in several days if that. The steady stream of smoke rising above his head from his cigar made her cough a little and she dropped into the chair beside him.

"Hey, what's she doing here?" barked one of the players. "This ain't a lady's game."

She leaned forward and forced a smile. "Well, maybe I ain't a lady!"

Roars of laughter rose from the men.

"She's my good luck charm," the young one said. "Leave her alone; she stays!"

They scowled at Trixie, but he ignored them and tossed a twenty-dollar gold piece onto the table.

"Why don't you get us a round of drinks, honey," he said to her. "And keep 'em coming."

"Who should I tell the bartender the drinks are for?" she asked, dipping her finger under his chin and smiling.

"You can call me Lucky," he said. "And this here's Boyd, Cooper, and Grady. Bring us a bottle of Red-Eye, and you can keep the change."

She smiled, knowing she had them in the palm of her hand. "I'll be back with the drinks in just a minute, fellas."

She went to the bar, making sure she didn't get too close to Willy, who was there to keep an eye on her in case of trouble. Minutes later, she was back at the table with the bottle and four glasses.

Lucky looked at her. "Ain't you drinking with us?"

Her heart raced; she'd never touched any of the drinks she served her customers. Though it made her nervous when they invited her to indulge, she'd always managed to talk her way out of it.

She feigned a smile. "I wouldn't want to drink up all your whiskey," she said, using her signature excuse. "Then there wouldn't be enough for you and them guys."

"I don't mind sharing," Cooper said with a smile. "You can even sit with me!"

Lucky slammed his hand on the table, and Trixie noticed Willy flinch from the corner of her eye; he rested his hand on his gun.

"I saw her first," Lucky said. "If anyone is gonna share with her, it'll be me."

Trixie waved a friendly hand at him and giggled as sincerely as she could muster. "Red Eye is a man's drink," she said, making another attempt at discouraging them to force the whiskey on her. "I'd prefer sarsaparilla."

Lucky dipped into his pocket once more and pulled out two bits. "Here, honey, go get yourself a bottle of sarsaparilla."

She took the money with a giggle and went to the bar for the drink. When she returned, she resumed her place next to Lucky and allowed him to put his arm around her; it made her cringe, but it was the only way she was going to get information out of him.

"Ante up!" Lucky said.

Each man put a silver dollar in the center of the table, and Lucky dealt the cards. Trixie leaned back in her chair and paid attention to her bottle of sarsaparilla, sipping from it and keeping her ears open for any information that would prove helpful in bringing together Willy's plan.

Lucky examined his cards and tossed another silver dollar in the *kitty.*

"Hey," Cooper complained. "What do you think this is; payday?"

"No," he barked at his friend. "But tomorrow is, so stop jawing and put your money in or fold."

"What if we don't get paid tomorrow?" Boyd complained.

"Why wouldn't we?" Lucky asked.

Cooper looked up from his cards. "I heard Dead-eye Jack is in these parts waiting for the payroll, so he can rob the stage after it leaves Carson's Ridge Way Station; then none of us is gonna git paid."

Trixie's ears perked up.

"Two of Dead-eye Jack's gang swung from the end of a rope last month, and he won't pull that job alone," Lucky said.

"Where'd you hear that?" Boyd asked.

"It was in the Tombstone Epitaph, dummy!" Lucky said with a chuckle. "You'd know that if any of you could read."

Boyd scooted his chair back and let it fall behind him. "Who are you calling dummy?" he asked, gritting his teeth.

Trixie slowly rose from her chair and backed away; she'd gotten every bit of information she was going to get from them, and she knew by experience that a fight was about to break out. She took that as her cue to get out of the way.

With her tip money jingling in her pocket, she ran up the stairs just after the first punch was thrown, and she didn't stop until she reached her room at the end of the hall. Willy had run out just before the fight started and had gone up the back steps in the alley and met her at her door.

"Let's get out of here!" he said. "I heard everything he said; I knew Dead-eye Jack was trying to get his hands on that payroll, and I aim to get it before he does!"

Trixie packed her things quickly, and they went down the back stairs and through the alley toward Willy's hotel at the end of the block where the rest of the gang waited on them.

Beatrix walked through town toward the crowd that had gathered in front of the sheriff's office where she was supposed to meet with him. He'd sent word to her by messenger just before he was due to pick her up for lunch, excusing himself because of a robbery. The note had asked her to meet him at his office at two o'clock, and as she neared the jail, it seemed he was nowhere around, but outside his office was swarming with angry men.

The closer she came to the crowd, the more shouting she heard.

"Get the ropes ready," one bystander shouted. "When the posse returns, we're gonna have a lynching party!"

Whooping and hollering from the crowd continued until she approached and one of the men pointed to her.

"There's the girl; get her!"

Two big men charged toward her and grabbed her before she could get away from them.

"Gotcha, Trixie," one of them shouted.

"Let me go!" she squealed, but they tightened their grip on her arm.

"Yeah, that's Trixie," another one shouted from the back of the crowd. "She was with them outlaws when they shot Buford!"

"No!" she cried. "I'm not Trixie."

"That's what name you gave us last night in the saloon!"

She sucked in her breath with a loud gasp.

"I've *never* stepped one foot inside of a saloon!" she squealed.

"Well you did last night b'cause I danced with you, myself!"

"I did too—you danced with me *twice!"*

"Let me go," she whined. "I didn't dance with any of you. It must have been someone else."

"Unless you've got a twin sister," one of them said. "It was you in there dancing and singing half the night."

"I'm an only child!" she said.

"Then it was you in the saloon, and you who was with the outlaws—and you who's gonna swing from a tree by the neck if you don't start telling us where your gang run off to with our money!"

"I didn't do anything; I'm innocent," she cried.

"That's what they all say," someone yelled from the crowd.

"I say we string her up right now!" another one said.

"Please," she cried. "You have to believe me; it wasn't me!"

"Let's hang her!"

"Yeah, get the ropes!"

"Help!" Beatrix screamed.

Sheriff Muley waded through the crowd and shoved the men aside. "Let her go!" he demanded.

"We aim to hang her," one of them said. "She's the girl from the saloon; Buford recognized her from last night. He said she was there with them outlaws when they robbed the stage this morning and took our payroll and shot ole Bu."

"Don't listen to them, Sheriff," Beatrix pleaded. "I was at the boarding house this morning; you can ask Miss Mavis. I had breakfast with her."

"She's lying!" Cooper shouted. "We all saw her in the saloon singing last night; she was playing cards with Lucky and me. Boyd and Grady were there too; they can identify her and so can Buford."

"That's right," Lucky said, stepping to the front of the crowd. "That's her! I bought her a sarsaparilla! She ran off when me and Boyd started fighting."

"It wasn't me in the saloon," Beatrix said. "I was having dinner with the sheriff at the Palace Restaurant last night."

"You're a liar, Trixie!" Lucky said. "The sheriff wouldn't have dinner with you!"

"My name is not Trixie!" she cried. "I did have dinner with the sheriff." She turned to Sheriff Muley looking to him to back her up, but he wasn't saying a word. "Tell them!"

Her heart sank to her feet that felt as flat as a hotcake. Sheriff Muley took her by the arm and led her toward the jailhouse. "I'm afraid these men are right," he said, soberly. "I'm going to have to hold you until we can sort this out."

"But you know I'm innocent!" she cried.

"That's what they all say, Trixie!" Lucky shouted.

Beatrix went along with the sheriff; her heart was broken, and her spirit was crushed. How could he go along with them after the wonderful dinner they'd had? She thought they had at least become friends. Who would help her now if not the sheriff?

"Wait just a minute, Sheriff," someone called out from behind them.

Mr. Wallaby followed them into the jailhouse, and he closed the door against the crowd that was still hollering about lynching her.

"You need to leave, Wallaby!" the sheriff warned him. "This is not your business."

"It is my business because she's my betrothed; I have a contract, remember?"

"I'm not discussing this right now," the sheriff growled. "I have to put a posse together and find whoever robbed the stage this morning and shot one of the drivers."

"But I can help, Sheriff," Mr. Wallaby said with a gleam in his eye.

"Unless you plan to join the posse, there isn't anything you can do to fix this."

Mr. Wallaby smiled as he stared at Beatrix, making her feel uncomfortable.

"I have money saved," he began. "I was going to use it to build a house for my bride, but I'll give it to the miners to cover their lost wages."

"Those men got away with about five thousand dollars!" the sheriff said. "I don't think you have that kind of money."

"I do!" he said. "I've been saving my entire life, and I put away the inheritance when my parents passed away. I'll pay for their loss if Miss Beatrix agrees to be my bride." He smiled at her, and it made her cringe. "Granted, with no money for a proper home, we'll have to remain in the small room at the back of the schoolhouse, but it's better than the sheriff's jail—and certainly better than swinging from a tree!" He took a step toward her, and she cowered behind the sheriff. "I'm even willing to forget your trip to the saloon; all you have to do is honor your contract with me and become my bride and I'll make all of this go away."

"Lock me up, Sheriff!" Beatrix demanded.

# SEVEN

Trixie slowed her horse to a light canter, thinking she'd heard another set of hooves clip-clopping against the trail behind her. She slowly turned her head, but no one was there; was she hearing things? Being the lookout for the others had her spooked. She hadn't signed up for this; all she wanted was her cut so she could be on her way. Willy had forced her to backtrack along the trail to make sure they hadn't been followed, and to alert them if the sheriff was forming a posse to come after them.

They were held up at the way station at Carson's Ridge, and if she wasn't back by supper time, they'd be moving further south toward the border of Mexico—with or without her.

Willy had refused to give her any of the money, claiming that if he held onto it, his gang would stick with him. It was the way they'd always handled things. She knew she wasn't the first saloon girl to assist him with a robbery, and she wouldn't be the last. Seeing that this might be her only chance to work with Willy and his gang, she would follow his instructions to the letter. She needed that money to get out of the life that was suffocating her and making an old woman out of her. She wanted a husband and a family; no man would consider her for such a future if she didn't straighten up her life and get out of the saloon.

She had everything planned out. She would move to another town, and she would tell any potential suitors that she'd inherited her father's fortune. The only problem was, she had no father as far as she knew. Every time she'd asked her mother, the only thing she would tell her beside his name, was that her father was dead. After her mother's death, she'd done some poking around and found old newspaper archives that told of her father's hanging for robbery and murder. She supposed she'd inherited at least the robbery trait from the man, so in a way, her story would have some merit. Being the daughter of a thief and a murderer had earned her the trust of Wild Willy Wilcox, who came from a similar background. He'd told her it was *in their blood* to be bad, and they couldn't help but steal from others.

She knew it was an excuse for her behavior, but she was desperate to turn her life around, and she didn't see any other way. Working in the saloon had put a roof over her head and food in her belly. She'd tried to save her money to get away from the saloons, but someone had found her stash of money and stolen it from her, leaving her feeling discouraged to the point of giving up.

She kept moving, despite the hair on the back of her neck prickling. Someone was following her but who could it be? Whoever it was, he was staying far enough behind her to keep out of sight. She'd been out there for a couple of hours wandering around the area but hadn't seen a soul in the wilderness. The trousers Willy had lent her were chafing her legs, and her seat was sore, but she was determined to do as he asked, or he would refuse her a share of the payroll.

A sudden noise from behind her startled her, and before she could get out of the way, a man had jumped onto her horse from a tree branch and had his hand around her belly.

She let out a scream, and the horse tried to take off running from the jolt of extra weight on his back, but her captor managed to stop him by pulling excessively on the bridle.

He yanked his head up. "Whoa, boy!"

The horse came to a complete stop, and the jumper slid from the rear, yanking Trixie down with him, and she tried to pull her arm away, but he twisted it behind her and pinned her up against the tree. She peered up into his face, a black patch covering his left eye, and a long scar down his left cheek.

"You're hurting me! Who are you and what do you want?" Trixie demanded. "I have nothing to steal so you can be on your way and leave me alone."

He pulled his pearl-handled pistol from his holster and stuffed it under her chin. "Shut your trap and undo your gun belt and throw it to the side."

She reached slowly for the buckle with her free hand and loosened it, then tossed it as far away from her as she could.

"Now you're going to tell me where Wild Willy went with my money from the stage robbery or I'm going to hang you from that tree I just jumped from."

Her breath hitched, and tears trickled down her cheeks. "Who are you?"

"Jack's the name; Dead-eye Jack!"

Her breath hitched again; she'd heard about him from the miners and had asked Willy about

109

him last night. He'd told her how dangerous he was, and if he caught up to them, he'd kill them all.

Jack shook Trixie. "If you don't tell me where Willy and his gang went with my money," he said through gritted teeth. "This face is the last one you'll ever see."

No amount of money was worth her life, and she did not owe Willy any loyalty; he owed her a cut of the money he'd promised her.

Jack gave her another shake and pulled back the hammer on his gun.

"Carson's Ridge," she blurted, her voice shaky. "The way station."

He snatched the rope from the ground that he intended to hang her with and pushed her against the tree. "Hold out your arms in front of you," he said.

She flailed herself all over trying to break loose from him. "You said if I told you where Willy was you'd let me go!" she cried.

"Not just yet," he said. "I'm going to tie you to this tree, and if I don't find Willy when I get to the way station, I'm going to come back and hang you from the tree!"

"No!" she pleaded with him. "Please let me go; I'm not lying. I'll even go with you."

"You'll only slow me down," he said, wrapping the rope around her hands and then around her middle. After she was bound tightly, he wrapped the rope around the tree several times and tied it around the back of the tree, far out of her reach. "That should hold you for a while; if I don't come back, I'm sure someone will find you in a couple of days—unless the wolves get to you first."

Trixie screamed, but he threw his head back and laughed and then mounted her horse, leaving her there screaming and calling out to him to cut her loose, but he didn't look back.

Sheriff Muley finished interviewing both drivers of the stage and then went back to the jailhouse where his deputy guarded Beatrix in the cell. He didn't like holding her there, but he had no other choice; it was the only way to keep her safe from the angry mob of men waiting to hang her for a crime he didn't believe she had any way of committing. Though the facts were a little muddled, he had to admit; the evidence was becoming stacked against her.

As he approached the jailhouse, the townspeople crowded around him asking him questions all at once.

He held up his hand to quiet them. "I'm working on it; I'll let you know as soon as I get everything straightened out. You'll get your justice and your money back; I give you my word."

He turned his back on the crowd and went inside the jailhouse, barring the door behind him.

"How's the prisoner?" he asked the deputy when he walked into the office. A door separated his office from the jail, and he didn't want Beatrix knowing he was back in his office just yet. He had to put together a timeline of the facts before he forgot important details.

"I think she's still pacing the floor," his deputy said. "If you're back, I'll go out and check the roundup for the posse. We ought to have at least fifty men by now."

"Hurry back and let me know."

The deputy nodded and left the building. Sheriff Muley bolted the door after the deputy left and sat back down at his desk to write out the timeline the judge would need for the inquest hearing.

His thoughts wandered to his dinner companion from last night; Beatrix did not fit the part of a thief or murderer. She'd been raised properly and was educated. Her look-alike, Trixie, had been described by the men in the saloon last night as being crass and not well-spoken, and she wore a couple of six-guns at her waist. He'd taken away Beatrix's Derringer she claimed belonged to her father and then whined about it being her only form of defense. He'd checked with the gunsmith in town, and he hadn't had a sale in four days so that ruled out the possibility she might have purchased another firearm when he refused to return her Derringer.

He recalled his brief interview with Hal, the bartender at the Silver Dollar Saloon. The one they called Trixie, had hired on at the saloon at four o'clock yesterday and hadn't come down to the bar until nine o'clock to sing her first number and serve a few drinks before sitting down to a poker game with Lucky, who claimed to have mentioned getting paid the following day. He'd even mentioned they'd heard rumors at the mine that Dead-eye Jack was bragging that he was going to rob the stage of its payroll after it left Carson's Ridge Way Station. The sheriff wondered if he was involved since the stage was robbed several miles before the way station. Both stage drivers recognized Trixie as coming in on the afternoon stage yesterday but thought it was odd that the same woman had come in on the stage the day before. That woman would be Beatrix. How had she managed to slip out of town and travel all the way back to Bisbee to catch the stage again the following day? It wasn't possible, was it?

Sheriff Muley propped his elbows on his desk and thought about the final piece to the puzzle—the part that baffled him the most. He'd had dinner with Beatrix last night and hadn't taken her home until eight o'clock, which would have given her plenty of time to change and get back to the saloon in time for her first song by nine o'clock. He'd checked with Miss Mavis, and she'd backed up her story about getting breakfast at the boarding house, but that she'd served it at seven o'clock this morning and hadn't seen Beatrix again until she went out at two o'clock to meet with him at the jail. Her alibi was not as iron-clad as he'd hoped, and it worried him about his involvement with the beautiful young woman.

Had he fallen in love with a common thief—saloon girl disguised as a school teacher?

# EIGHT

Sheriff Muley told the men to split up into teams of ten men each and for each team to pick a trail leading away from town in all directions. Since he'd shown them a few Wanted posters, Wild Willy had been recognized as being in the saloon last night, but Dead-eye Jack had not been spotted. At least with Wild Willy Wilcox, the sheriff had some idea of what he was dealing with; he had a reputation for roaming from one territory to another leaving a trail of disgruntled saloon girls behind whom he'd used to get information from drunken miners, promising them a cut of the robbery, but never followed through with that promise. Beatrix was not in any hurry to leave jail and go after what would be *her cut*, so he had to believe her story. If she was indeed leading a double life as a saloon girl named Trixie, surely, she would have never gone to jail to avoid marrying Mr. Wallaby. She would have used the schoolmaster to free her, so she could go after Wild Willy herself. That alone was what convinced him of her innocence; now all he had to do was to prove it.

He was convinced Beatrix had nothing to do with the robbery, but he hadn't yet figured out why all the evidence kept pointing back to her. Was it possible someone was framing her to take the fall?

He and his deputy split up and each took one of the trails that led to the Carson's Ridge Way Station, the sheriff taking the narrowest and most likely trail. He figured the best way to catch the outlaws was to backtrack to where the robbery happened. He was an excellent tracker and could follow any trail. He counted on those skills to lead him to Wild Willy and the payroll money.

He followed the narrow trail, keeping his eyes wide and his ears perked for any sign there might be trouble afoot. From a distance, he could hear the faint cry from a woman. He looked up ahead and behind to see if there was anyone around, but he didn't see anyone. He went slowly down the trail a little further, when he realized she was calling out for help.

Mindful that it could be a trap, he continued cautiously down the trail. When he rounded the bend, he saw a woman tied to a tree out in the middle of a grassy area to the side of the trail. He surveyed the area noting he could see for some distance in either direction and there was no one there besides the woman.

When she spotted him, she cried out even louder. "Help me!"

His heart ticked like the second hand on his pocket watch as he neared her. Even from that distance, he could see the deep resemblance to Beatrix.

*Gotcha, Trixie!*

He nudged the flank of his mount urging him to gallop so he could get to the woman before whoever tied her there would come back for her.

His horse skidded in the grass when he pulled back on the reins bringing him to an abrupt stop just short of the tree. He slid from his mount and rushed to her side, but his gaze fell on the gun belt with a couple of six guns that lay in the grass only a few feet from her. He bent to pick it up and slung it over his saddle horn. Then he removed the guns and tucked them away in his saddle bags and buckled the straps.

"Hurry and untie me," Trixie squealed. "Dead-eye Jack is going to come back and hang me!"

"Are you Trixie?" he asked, walking around the tree.

She scowled. "How did you know my name?"

"I've met your twin in Tombstone!" he said, reaching for the rope to untie her from the tree.

"How could you?" she asked. "I'm an only child."

Sheriff remembered hearing Beatrix say the same thing. Was it possible they were separated at birth? It wasn't uncommon.

"Do you happen to know where you were born?" the sheriff asked, working the rope to loosen it.

"El Paso, Texas," she said, annoyance obvious in her tone. "Why are you asking me such silly questions? Dead-eye Jack is gonna be back here any minute to kill me!"

"I have one more for you," he said holding onto the rope before unwinding it from her wrists. "Did you help Wild Willy Wilcox rob the Wells Fargo stage coach this morning?"

"I was there but I didn't help," she cried. "I swear I didn't know he was gonna shoot the driver; is he dead?"

"He's lost a lot of blood, but the doc thinks he can patch him up as good as new," the sheriff answered. "I'm going to have to take you back to Tombstone for the inquest hearing, but if you can help us catch Wild Willy and Dead-eye Jack, the judge will be lenient with you. Just being there during the robbery makes you an accomplice and you can spend some time in the territorial prison."

She gasped. "I can't go to prison; please, I'll tell you whatever you want."

"I'll take you back to town so you can have a witness there when I take your statement, but we need to hurry. It'll be dark soon, but I'm sure their trail is getting cold."

"No!" she squealed. "He's waiting for me at the way station at Carson's Ridge."

"You don't really think he's there waiting for you, do you?"

"He better be, or Dead-eye Jack will be coming back for me. He told me he'd hang me from this tree if Willy wasn't at the way station."

"How long ago did he tie you to this tree?" Sheriff Muley asked her.

"I don't know; maybe an hour."

"We better hurry," he warned her.

No sooner had he said it than he heard a horse galloping at full speed toward them from the direction of Carson's Ridge.

Sheriff Muley scooped Trixie up in his arms and slung her onto the saddle, then threw his leg up over behind her and kicked at the horse's flank to make him gallop.

"Hurry," Trixie squealed.

Gunshots rent the air and Sheriff Muley leaned over Trixie to guard her from stray bullets as he pushed the horse faster toward town.

# NINE

Sheriff Muley pushed the horse as much as he could with two riders, though it wasn't fast enough to outrun bullets. As soon as he rounded the bend, he stopped the horse and pushed him and Trixie around the tree and into the brush. Then he pulled out his gun and prepared to shoot at whatever came around the curve in the trail. Shots still fired, and when the horse approached, he could see the man with the eye patch galloping toward them. He aimed for the rider's shoulder and pulled the trigger; down he went, but the horse continued toward the sheriff. He held up a hand to keep from spooking the horse, hoping to stop him.

"Whoa boy," he said, reaching out toward the walking horse. He blew out through his nostrils, his breathing just as hard as the sheriff's horse. Grabbing for the reins, Sheriff Muley managed to calm the horse and tie him to the brush near his own horse. Then he cautiously walked back toward the outlaw knowing he could be playing opossum even though he was lying face-down in the grass. Sheriff Muley crept closer, his gun drawn and ready, but the man didn't move. When he was upon him, he sighted his gun and picked it up. He approached the outlaw slowly.

"On your feet, Jack," Sheriff Muley said.

Dead-eye Jack rolled over and groaned. His shoulder was bleeding, but he rose to his feet with a lot of trouble. The sheriff positioned himself behind his prisoner and urged him toward his horse.

Trixie squealed when she saw Dead-eye Jack. "You were coming back to hang me, weren't you?"

Jack looked up at her on the sheriff's horse and growled. "I'd have done it if the sheriff hadn't winged me; you lied to me!"

"Don't talk," Sheriff Muley warned Jack. "It'll only make things worse for you. Get up on your horse."

Sheriff Muley waited for the groaning outlaw to mount and then pulled out his handcuffs and tossed them up to him.

"Put them on."

Jack hesitated until the sheriff pulled back the hammer of his gun and trained it on him. "Would you like a bullet in the other shoulder?"

"You wouldn't shoot an unarmed man, would you?" Jack asked coyly.

"Not normally, no, but you're my prisoner, and you're resisting arrest! Do you want me to take you into town to see the saw-bones or do you want to die out here of lead poisoning?"

Dead-eye Jack put the cuffs on his wrists despite the pain from his shoulder that made him groan.  The sheriff reached for the reins of Jack's horse and led him closer to his own horse and then mounted.

Jack and Trixie eyed each other, but the sheriff held up his gun. "No talking until we get back into town; you'll have plenty of opportunity to talk then."

Sheriff Muley steered the horses toward town; it was going to be a long and dusty ride back, but he'd gotten the girl and one of the outlaws. How was he going to break the news to the unhappy miners that he hadn't recovered their money yet? Worse than that, how was he going to explain about Trixie to Beatrix, and Beatrix to Trixie when he didn't understand it himself?

Sheriff Muley rode into town with both his prisoners in tow; thankfully, the rest of the posse was still out searching, or there would have been a mob waiting for them. The deputy came in from the other trail empty-handed.

He immediately spotted the sheriff and slid from his mount to help him bring in the two prisoners.

He took one look at Trixie and pointed at her with confusion in his expression. "Hey, isn't she already in jail?"

"No," the sheriff said. "I'll explain it to you in a minute; except that I don't really understand it myself. First, I need you to take him in and then run down and get the saw-bones to fix up his shoulder."

Inside the jailhouse, the deputy took Dead-eye Jack to a cell in the back, while the sheriff kept Trixie up front.

Once the deputy had Jack securely locked up, he exited the back of the jail, his expression even more confused, if that was possible. He paused to look at Trixie once more before leaving the office to fetch the doctor.

Sheriff Muley sat Trixie down in the chair opposite his desk and untied the rope from her hands and her waist.

"Ain't you gonna take me back to the jail?" she asked, wringing her red wrists.

Sheriff Muley noticed the difference in her speech compared to Beatrix right away. It also puzzled him that their names were so similar.

"Is your full name Beatrix?" he asked.

"Yeah; how did you know that?"

"I'll ask the questions!" he said, firmly.

She threw her hands up and slouched in the chair, the men's trousers she was wearing made her look even less like a lady than she should. He almost felt sorry for her.

"Did you come here from El Paso?"

She shook her head. "The Barbary Coast. Why are you so interested in El Paso?"

Knowing Beatrix was from El Paso, he had to wonder if it was possible they had been separated at birth. They were too identical in appearance not to be twins.

"Do you have any family in El Paso?"

"Just my pa, but he's dead."

"When is your birthday?"

She folded her arms and scoffed at him. "What's with all the weird questions? Don't you want to know about Wild Willy?"

"Yes, of course," he said, realizing he'd let her likeness to Beatrix distract him from his job. "Tell me where he is, and I'll spare you hanging in case Buford, the driver who got shot during the robbery, doesn't live."

"That wasn't my idea!" she said. "I didn't shoot the driver; why should I hang for what Willy did?"

"Because you were with him, and in the Arizona territory it's against the law to be along with someone when they murder someone; it's called being an accessory to the crime. You were an accomplice just by being there, and you can get hanged for that."

"Willy and his gang said they were going to wait for me at the way station, but they lied to me!" she said angrily.

"How many are in his gang?"

"Four, besides him, so five total," she said, listing off their names.

Sheriff Muley wrote them down on his pad; he recognized two of the names because he had recent dodgers for them.

"Where were they headed, do you know?"

Trixie shrugged. "Willy said if I didn't get back in time they would be heading south toward the border of Mexico, but since he lied to me, he could be anywhere."

"Maybe," the sheriff started to say.

The deputy knocked at the door and Sheriff Muley let him and the doctor in, bolting the door behind them. "Go on back, Doc," the deputy said to him, handing him the key.

When he was back behind closed doors, Sheriff Muley turned to his deputy. "Round up the men who've come back and send them out to Carson's Ridge."

"But I just came back from there, and I didn't see any sign of them," the deputy argued.

"And Dead-eye Jack was just there and didn't find them either," Trixie chimed in.

"I know," the sheriff said. "But I have a hunch; comb the area around the way station. There's a wooded area just behind with a small cave; I have a feeling that's where they're hiding out."

"I didn't go out that far," the deputy admitted. "I'll get the men and go right away, but we won't get there before dark. We'll have to take torches."

"Don't light them until you get right on the cave," the sheriff warned. "It's a full moon tonight so you should be able to see up to that point."

The deputy left the office to do the sheriff's bidding, leaving him to finish his interview with Trixie.

He set his pen down and leaned back in his chair. "I have someone I'd like you to meet," he said pointing back toward the jail. "But she's in my jail for mistaken identity."

"Mistaken identity?" Trixie asked. "Who did they think she was?"

"You!" the sheriff said, rising from his chair.

"Me?" Trixie squealed. "What are you talking about?"

He dug out a pair of handcuffs from his desk drawer and cuffed her to the chair she was seated in.

"What's this for?"

"I'm going in the back." He held up a finger. "Hold on a minute; I need to prepare your cellmate. I'll be right back."

"Cellmate? Why are you locking me up?"

"I'm going to tell you the same thing I told her; it's for your own good. I have to keep you here until we get the outlaws back here and we can have an inquest hearing."

He opened the door to the back and closed the door behind him. He stopped at the first cell where Dead-eye Jack was hollering so loudly it echoed in the large open area.

He poked his head inside the doorway. "Do you need some help, Doc?"

"I'm almost done," he answered. "I gave him a sedative but not enough to knock him out. I think he's going to live."

"Good, then he can stand trial for threatening to hang Trixie!"

At the mention of the name Trixie, Beatrix rushed to the front of her cell and grappled onto the bars. "Trixie? What about Trixie? Did you find the real one?"

Her voice sounded anxious, and it made Sheriff Muley even more nervous to tell her about the girl who looked just like her.

"Yes, I found her tied to a tree where that man intended to come back and hang her, but there's more," he said cautiously.

He stood in front of Beatrix and put the key in the lock, making a note of the worry in her eyes.

"Before I bring her back here, I need to tell you a few things."

Beatrix backed away from the bars, her hands drawing up toward her open mouth to disguise the gasp. "What is it?"

"The girl I have out there," he began. "Well, her name is also *Beatrix.*"

Another gasp and her eyes widened. Sheriff Muley opened the cell door and went to her, steering her toward the cot in the corner of the cell. "She's a dead ringer for you, too, I have to admit."

"She is? How?"

"I was hoping you could tell me a little more about your childhood that could explain the likeness between the two of you."

"There isn't anything to tell. I don't have any siblings, and I don't have any cousins. I was raised in the same house where I was born. Coming to Tombstone is the first time I've ever traveled. And speaking of traveling; my father is due on the stage tomorrow; can you please let me out of here now that you found the real Trixie?"

"I'm afraid it's not that easy," the sheriff said. "I'm going to need to hold you both here until we get Wild Willy Wilcox in custody. Then I can let you go for sure, and we might have to wait until I hear the rest of the story until I can let Trixie—the other Beatrix go."

"What are the odds of another woman looking like me and having my same name?"

"Is it possible you could be twins—separated at birth?" he asked with caution.

"No! My mother would never have gotten rid of her child. My mother told me about how many she miscarried before having me, and how much she wished she could have given me a sibling. She almost died the night she had me, and a week later, the doctor had to remove her uterus with surgery because she wouldn't stop bleeding. I'm an only child—unless you count the siblings that never made it."

"I'm sorry to hear that," he said.

She drew in a breath and looked into the sheriff's eyes, her green eyes full of fear.

"Let's get this over with before I lose my nerve!"

The sheriff chuckled and pulled her into a hug. "I think everything is going to work out just fine. Don't worry; I'll be right here if you need me."

She felt good in his arms, and not just because he no longer had to worry about her being a saloon girl named Trixie, but because he realized he loved her no matter what.

He pulled away from her despite how badly he wanted to keep her there and went out into his office to get Trixie. He passed by the outlaw's cell and noticed the doctor had left the sleeping man alone and had locked him in his cell.

When he entered his office from the back, he saw the doctor putting on his jacket and put up a hand for him to wait.

"Can I get your help with her a minute?"

The doctor looked at Trixie and cocked his head to the side. "Are you ill, dear?" he asked her.

"No, she's not ill, but I'm about to take her back to the cell with the other one, and I might need your help."

"What?" Trixie asked. "Are you afraid I'm gonna try to run off when I see the girl you claim looks just like me?"

"No!" the sheriff rebutted. "But women tend to *faint* easily, and this could cause some shock."

Trixie smirked. "Look, Sheriff, I'm as tough as they come. I ain't never fainted in my life; I ain't some dainty little girl."

"Well, come along then," he said. "But humor me and cover your face and let the doc lead you until I tell you that it's alright to look."

"You're not feeding me to a bear or something, are you? B'cause you're starting to scare me a little."

The sheriff chuckled. "What happened to that tough girl?"

"Fine!" she said covering her face.

The doctor led her into the back; her handcuffed hands over her face. The sheriff walked ahead and opened the cell door and stood near Beatrix.

"Don't look until I tell you," he warned.

She kept her head down until the doctor had Trixie inside the cell in front of them.

"Alright, you can look."

Both girls looked up slowly and both let out a scream and down they went. The doc caught Trixie, while the sheriff caught Beatrix.

"I knew this was a bad idea!" he said.

# TEN

Sheriff Muley startled awake when the door to the office opened. He stretched and looked at the clock above the door that told him he'd been asleep for about two hours. It was a little after midnight, and his deputy looked just as worn out as he felt as the man walked into the office and sat down. The sheriff went over to the coffee pot and poured himself a cup.

"You look like you've had a rough night!" the deputy said.

Sheriff Muley nodded.

"Well I have something that'll cheer you up," his deputy said. "You were right about them hiding out in the cave. The posse is bringing in Wild Willy and his gang. They're about a mile out; I thought I'd come and make sure you were ready for them."

"I have an empty cell back there. The doc and I moved the women to his office so he could keep an eye on them; they both fainted, so we had to move them."

"I'm guessing the reunion didn't go well?" the deputy asked.

"No! It went as badly as it could have, but I need to concentrate on getting the outlaws processed, and I have Mr. Pruett coming in on the stage tomorrow; I'll have to find a way to question him about Beatrix. Did you know they were both named Beatrix? Who would do that?"

"That's strange. What does Beatrix plan to do about Mr. Wallaby?" the deputy asked.

"Oh yes, that; I still have to address her complaint against Wallaby for fraud, and his complaint against Beatrix for breach of contract."

"Sounds to me like I'm going to have a mound of paperwork to do around here," the deputy said in a complaining tone.

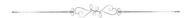

Sheriff Muley paced in front of the ticket office for the stage line and waited. The stage was due in at two o'clock, and it was already two-fifteen. He'd gone to see Beatrix and Trixie earlier that morning, and the two of them were getting along famously. It pleased the sheriff that they were working things out. Beatrix had even offered to help poor Trixie out of the mess she'd gotten herself into with the outlaws. They were still under the protection of the sheriff and being held in custody at the doctor's office since the jail was full, and the sheriff didn't want them out on the street until the judge arrived on the very stage he was waiting on—the stage Mr. Pruett was due on as well.

How would he break the news about Trixie to Mr. Pruett? Was it possible he already knew about the girl? Judging by the things Beatrix had said about him, he didn't seem like the secret-keeper the sheriff had wondered about, but he'd been known to be wrong before.

Finally, he could hear the horses galloping from a distance, the faint rumbling from the team drawing near. There was no preparing himself for the two men he would have to meet on that stage, so he took a deep breath and pasted on a half-smile when the stage rounded the buildings at the far end of town. As the stage came to a halt at the curb of the boardwalk in front of the ticket office, Muley took another deep breath and watched the porter drop the step-stool on the ground beneath the door so the passengers could exit the carriage.

He extended his hand to Judge Hendricks when he stepped foot on the boardwalk, greeting him with a firm handshake and a forced smile. Next, a man exited and looked around as if he was searching for someone to meet him.

"Are you looking for Beatrix?" the sheriff asked the older man.

"Yes, indeed, Sheriff," the man said.

"Which one?" Sheriff Muley asked.

"Pardon me?"

"Which Beatrix are you looking for?" the sheriff repeated himself.

The older man lowered his head. "I was afraid this would happen one day."

"Tell me everything," Sheriff Muley grilled Mr. Pruett. "Are the young ladies your real daughters?"

He hung his head as he shook it slowly. "My wife had given birth to another stillborn child, and there was a saloon girl named Verdie, who had traveled from town to our farm to see the midwife because the doctor had left town to be with a sick relative and no one knew when he'd come back. Verdie was accompanied by her co-worker at the saloon, a Miss Maxine. Verdie had been married, but her husband was hanged for robbery and murder just before the girls were born. My wife was devastated, and I knew the child she was birthing was our last hope of having a child. Just before Verdie died, she made Maxine promise to raise her child if anything happened to her, but when that first baby was born, Maxine panicked and gave the baby to my wife because she'd just given birth and the midwife couldn't revive the baby. Then, when Verdie gave birth to a second daughter, she decided to keep it because she died within minutes of birthing the second one. I'm ashamed to admit that I didn't want my wife to know that the babies were switched because she was so happy to have a child finally, I couldn't bear to break her heart. So, we buried my stillborn child with Verdie."

"Were any adoption papers ever filed?"

"No, I paid Maxine to leave town so my wife would never see that there was an identical twin because she knew she'd only given birth to one child that night. I knew that if the girls grew up in the same small town, the truth would come out. I gave her enough money to start all over again somewhere else and to raise the child right."

"How did they both come to be named Beatrix?" the sheriff asked.

"That was the name of Verdie's mother; Maxine made me promise to name the child after her real grandmother. I had no idea she would do the same with the other child."

"There's something else you should know," the sheriff began slowly. "The other Beatrix—she goes by Trixie, and she was involved in a stagecoach robbery with some known outlaws."

Mr. Pruett rose from the chair and paced the small space of the sheriff's office before standing in front of the barred window and looking out at the dusty town of Tombstone. "How did she get mixed up with them?"

"She met them in the saloon—where she was hired on as a singer and to serve drinks to the gentlemen."

"Oh no!" Mr. Pruett said. "What have I done? I was so worried about myself and my wife finding out I'd lied to her that I sent that poor child out into the world with another saloon girl. She had no chance at a normal life. I'm so ashamed that I paid her to leave town. I should have done more to help her care for the other child, and I should never have separated them. They deserved to grow up together, and I took that from them; how will my daughter ever be able to forgive me for sending away her sister? I never really thought they had a chance of finding each other."

"All you can do is tell them the truth and hope for the best," the sheriff said, hoping to encourage him. "If it helps any, they seem to be getting along quite nicely, and I believe they're happy they've met. They don't know they're twins, but I think they suspect it—we all did—it was the only logical explanation."

Mr. Pruett continued to stare out the window. "Funny that I've dreaded this day for twenty-one years, and now that it's here, I'm actually relieved. But I'll feel better when I know that my daughter doesn't hold it against me. What about the one who calls herself Trixie? Is Maxine here with her?"

"Sadly, Trixie has been without any adult supervision since she was fifteen—that's when the fever took Maxine."

Mr. Pruett's breath hitched as he turned to face the sheriff. "What has she been doing since then? Working in saloons?"

"I'm afraid so," the sheriff confirmed. "I believe that's why she got mixed up with Wild Willy and his gang. She's not the first saloon girl to get used as a decoy to rob a bank or the stage."

"That poor child," the older man said. "Can I see my daughter—can I see both of them?"

The sheriff nodded. "They're at the doctor's office; they fainted when they saw each other for the first time, but they're alright now. He's keeping them there until the judge has a chance to hold the inquest hearing. If we hurry, we can go over there and see them before the hearing starts."

# ELEVEN

"Daddy!" Beatrix said, flinging her arms around her father.

He hugged her with a sense of reserve. "I wasn't sure if you'd even want to see me."

He looked at Trixie, who stood to the side awkwardly.

Beatrix looked at her father sternly in the eye. "Of course I want to see you. I know there's a good explanation for the fact that Trixie and I look almost identical, and I'm hoping you'll tell me—

us—everything no matter how strange or painful it might be." She beckoned Trixie toward them. "Trixie and I talked, and the only thing we want to know right now is if we're really sisters?"

Mr. Pruett let out a chuckle of relief. "Yes! You're twins!"

She hugged her father again. "One more question, Daddy, and then we don't want to know anything else until we're ready to hear it; can I share you with Trixie because she doesn't have any parents?"

Mr. Pruett let out a half-laugh, half-cry, his lower lip quivering as he opened his other arm to Trixie. "Of course; it will be an honor to have two daughters."

Trixie joined them a little reluctantly, and they hugged until Trixie broke down and cried.

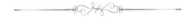

Judge Hendricks slammed his gavel down on the large desk inside the courtroom. "Order," he hollered. "I will not continue to have these

149

outbursts interrupting this inquest. Counsel, you may continue to cross-examine the witness."

Beatrix had loaned her a very conservative dress for the hearing, but she was so nervous sitting there, she felt completely exposed. Tears filled her eyes, and she dabbed at them with the handkerchief that Beatrix had lent her. The shouts from the onlookers had rattled her to her very core; how could they insist she be hanged when they'd already established it was Willy's gun that was likely the one that shot the driver? If only he'd owned up to it. She could, couldn't she? They'd made an oath to stick together if they got caught; they'd all agreed to keep quiet about the money. If they couldn't break them or get them to talk, there was nothing they could prove. That was what Willy had convinced them. But what if she told them everything? Would they kill her the way they claimed if the oath of loyalty was broken?

She had just taken the stand and had not had time to prepare for the many questions being thrown at her from the crowd. They were cruel at best, but her unprepared lawyer tried to help despite the fact they'd retained him only minutes before the inquest hearing.

"I'm sorry," she blurted out. "I know I shouldn't have helped Wild Willy and his gang; I regret going along with his plan to steal the money, but I know where he hid the money."

The crowded courtroom resounded with gasps and whispers that turned to discussions that grew louder by the minute.

She gulped. Her limbs shook, and her voice cracked, but she was determined to tell the judge everything. Willy and his gang had kept quiet about the money; they'd even denied they'd robbed the stage. So far, they'd all stuck together, and now, she had broken the pact. She'd done wrong, and now was the time to make it right. She'd been wrong in thinking that the money could give her a new start. Meeting her sister had given her a fresh outlook, and she did not want to lose that over stolen money and the guilt of watching Willy shoot a man. Thankfully, he was on the mend, but the angry crowd was still demanding a hanging party.

"Order," the judge hollered again. "Let the witness talk."

Trixie gazed into the angry face of Wild Willy and then at Dead-eye Jack. They both wanted to kill her; she could see it in their eyes. The very fact they would commit murder over money made her cringe.

Beatrix and her father had retained Charles Bodine as her lawyer, and now, he patiently waited for her to compose herself to finish her statement for the court.

"Take your time, Miss Donovan. We're all eager to hear where the money is."

"It's at an abandoned line shack about a mile back from the way station at Carson's Ridge. The well was dry, so Willy put it in the bucket and dropped it to the bottom of the well. He was going to reel it up after he was sure the posse didn't catch up to them. Then, they planned to cross the border of Mexico. Willy threatened to leave me if I didn't come back to tell them where the posse was headed, but he'd already decided they would stay low for a few days and hang around the way station in plain sight to make themselves look like they weren't guilty of the robbery."

"So the entire robbery was planned and premeditated?" Mr. Bodine asked.

"Yes!" Trixie answered.

"No further questions, Your Honor." Mr. Bodine said.

The judge slapped his gavel. "I believe this court should take a one-hour recess so the posse can go out to the line shack and see if they can recover the money. After that, I'm prepared to give my ruling on the matter."

Trixie stepped down from the chair beside the judge and rushed to Beatrix who opened her arms to her sister. "You were so brave," Beatrix said. "I'm proud to call you my sister."

# TWELVE

Sheriff Muley slapped at the reins of the rented carriage, Beatrix seated beside him. It was a nice evening for a ride out of the rowdy town. He planned to take her to the covered bridge just outside of town so they could listen to the trickling of the water from the stream while enjoying the nearly full moon and bright stars. After their talk in Mr. Bodine's office not ten minutes ago, he had a question weighing on his mind, and he aimed to ask her.

He steered the horse toward the covered bridge and parked in the grass to the side and hopped out. He helped Beatrix down from the carriage and tucked her hand in the crook of his elbow. Her shoes clicked against the wooden bridge in perfect time with the jingling of his spurs and it gave him time to think of how to word the question that weighed heavily on his mind.

Charles had informed him that marriage to another man would void her contract for marriage that seemed to be iron-clad, but it would not avert the lawsuit pending against her for breach of contract. He didn't mind; he would gladly give the disgruntled schoolmaster everything he owned in exchange for Beatrix's freedom.

He took Beatrix's hand in his and knelt. Her breath hitched, and she smiled. "I don't expect a proposal," she said.

"I know you don't," he said. "But if you'll have me, I'd like to marry you. Not because you need a husband to get you out of the contract, but because I fell in love with you the moment I saw you get off the stagecoach a few days ago."

Tears filled her eyes. "I feel the same way!"

He looked up at her and smiled, her green eyes glowing in the moonlight. "Will you do me the honor of becoming my wife?"

She giggled. "Yes!"

He rose from bended knee and pulled her into his arms. When his lips met hers, the crickets' song played like an orchestra of violins especially for them.

Beatrix and Trixie stood at the end of the boardwalk and watched Mr. Wallaby board the stagecoach out of town. He'd relinquished the teaching position, and the sheriff had arranged with the school board for Beatrix to take over and allow Trixie to be her assistant until she could earn her teaching certificate.

They'd settled in as roommates at the boarding house, and Beatrix's father had taken a room at the hotel. After the wedding, they would move out to the sheriff's ranch house, where her father would stay in the guestroom, but Trixie planned to stay at the boarding house to keep proper appearances. Her afternoon at the saloon was put behind her, and she was grateful she hadn't spent the night there. It would be tough enough to gain back the trust of the townspeople, and staying clear of the saloon was a start. Though it would be a tough adjustment to turn her life around, Beatrix had been a source of encouragement, as had her father, who had adopted her—albeit late in life—but better late than never.

She and Beatrix had stayed up late for the past two nights talking well into the wee hours of the morning, comparing favorites and telling stories of their lives. They had a lot of catching up to do.

Trixie sighed. "How am I going to pass for a proper lady? No one in this town is going to respect me, and I don't want to embarrass you at your wedding."

Beatrix couldn't help but notice how uncomfortable Trixie was in her borrowed dress and smiled. "Don't worry, my dear sister, we'll start by getting you some proper dresses."

"I believe a proper dress would help, but I need you to teach me how to be comfortable in them and teach me what you learned growing up. I need to know proper manners and how to act like a lady."

"It's not that difficult," Beatrix admitted. "The only thing you have to remember is that whatever urges you have to speak your mind or show your disapproval for something or someone, you simply suppress it. A proper lady knows how to keep her mouth shut in the company of others, no matter how much you want to express your own opinion."

"I don't know," Trixie said. "That seems like it would be so hard to do that I'd be screaming inside all the time."

Beatrix smiled. "That's how you know you're doing it right!"

They both giggled and hugged.

"It's going to be wonderful having a sister," Beatrix said.

Trixie nodded, a tear rolling down her cheek. "There's just one problem," she said. "Do we both have to go by Beatrix? That could get confusing!"

They laughed and hugged; yes, it was definitely going to be nice being sisters.

**THE END**

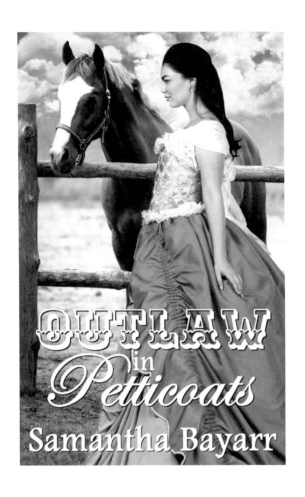

**Outlaw Petticoats HERE**

**The Reluctant Sheriff HERE**

## Preacher Outlaw

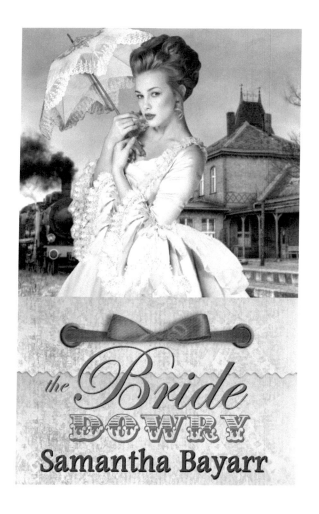

**The Bride Dowry HERE**

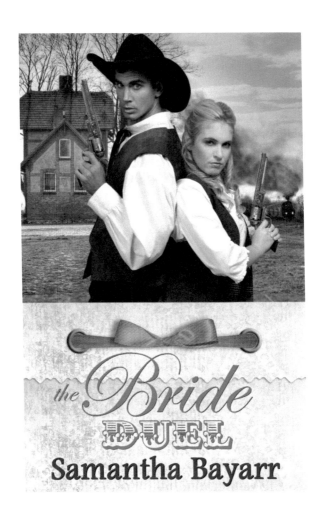

**Bride Duel HERE**

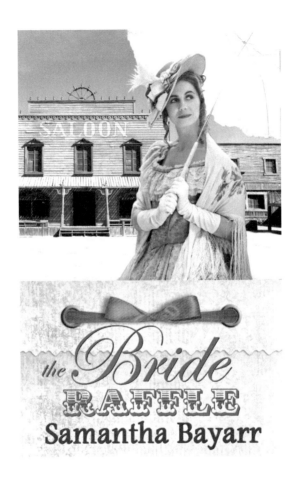

**Bride Raffle HERE**

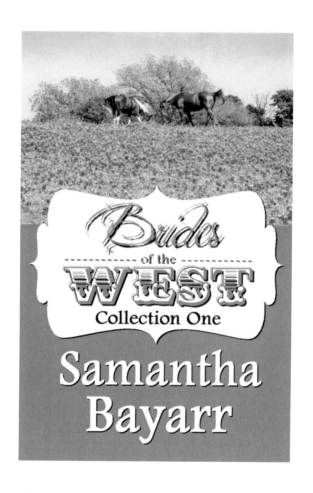

**Brides of the West Collection One HERE**

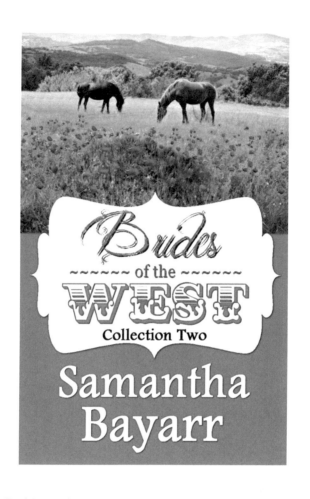

**Brides of the West Collection Two HERE**

# ABOUT THE AUTHOR

Samantha Bayarr, a former Paralegal, has written over 100 Christian Fiction Books in Contemporary Romance, Historical Romance, Western Romance, Amish Romance, and Amish Suspense.

She lives in an historical home in a small town in Florida with her husband, John Foster, who writes children's books. Samantha illustrates her husband's books, the first in the series entitled: Walla Walla and the Great Pirate Adventure. Check out these wonderful stories with a Christian message and over 50 full-color illustrations in each book.

 Facebook LIKE HERE

 Follow me on Twitter HERE

Follow me  on Pinterest HERE

 Follow my Blog HERE

Newly Released books
always FREE with
Kindle Unlimited.
♡ LOVE to Read?
♡ LOVE Discount Books?
♡ LOVE GIVEAWAYS?

## SIGN UP NOW
Click the Link Below to Join
my Exclusive Mailing List

**PLEASE CLICK HERE to SIGN UP!**